D1230760

THE
LIFE WE PRIZE

To Jandrun

by

ELTON TRUEBLOOD
Professor of Philosophy
Earlham College

Elton Trueblood

PRINIT PRESS, Publisher
Dublin, Indiana

THE LIFE WE PRIZE

Prinit Press Paperback Printing — Dec. 1981

First Word Paperback Printing — Nov. 1972

I.S.B.N. #0-932970-25-7

CONTENTS

THE LIFE WE PRIZE

PREFACE

In this book I have tried to draw, from a lifetime of thought and of study, what seems to me to be true on the central question of what kind of life man ought to live, whether in dark times or bright ones. Because we need all of the help that we can get, each must engage, in a disciplined effort, to try to discover whatever light may be available. Recognizing our own inadequacy, we must be humble enough to learn from the garnered wisdom of many centuries and of many different thinkers. It is not likely that the ideas represented in an honest book on this important subject will appear to be original. If they were original they would be highly suspect. It is inevitable, consequently, that nearly every sentence in such a book should sound platitudinous. This is a risk which I gladly run.

Most of the chapters which follow were written three decades ago. It is something of a surprise to discover that, for a paperback edition, little change is now required. Though some problems are more intense than they were a generation ago, the fundamental questions and the fundamental answers remain the same. If any reader wishes to compare the present edition with that published by the House of Harper in 1951, he will notice that the chief alteration occurs only in Chapter I. Some changes are required in the introductory chapter by the fact that, while the worst aspects of the Cold War have disappeared, other problems have presented themselves. The change in external affairs, nevertheless, has emphasized, rather than diminished, the importance of the task thus undertaken. The science of ethics, the one field of philosophical inquiry which is obviously self-justifying, has a pertinence now which is greater than it has had for several generations.

The title of this book came with unusual difficulty and was, in fact, not settled upon until the original galley proofs and even the page proofs had been corrected. The decision to choose this particular title came only when some of my friends made clear to me what I was trying to do. I was not, they helped me to see, describing the life which we demonstrate, since all of us fail in actual achievement. Instead, I was trying to describe a standard of conduct which is intrinsically self-validating. We cannot even know wherein we have failed, unless we recognize a standard by which to judge. Because, there is no other way to advance, whatever our failures and our successes may be, the standard is our most precious possession.

The writing of the first edition of *The Life We Prize* was accomplished in Charney Manor, said to be the oldest inhabited house of England. It was a genuine inspiration to try to think about the relevant truth for our stormy time while sitting in a room which has exposed oak beams seven hundred years old. We seek a wisdom appropriate to our time, but the fundamental problems and the fundamental solutions are not greatly different from those which faced men who sat under these same beams long ago. The beams have endured under strain, and so can men and women of our time, if the fundamental structure is sound.

E. T.

Earlham College

THE LIFE WE PRIZE

I

THE NECESSITY OF ETHICS

We are perpetually moralists.
—Samuel Johnson

No man knows what the future holds in any particular set of events, but every thoughtful person recognizes the probability that we shall live the remainder of our lives in turmoil. Whatever the course of history may be in the next few years, it will not be a course of tranquillity. Our modern world has developed so much animosity, so much justifiable fear, so much open conflict, that there is no guarantee of genuine peace. If the present tragic conflict were, by some developments now unforeseen, to come to a sudden end, it is reasonably certain that other conflicts, perhaps of equally tragic proportions, will arise. We are in the monsoon season of history, and we must learn to weather it out. Instead of pining for easier days, the way of wisdom lies in learning to live realistically in times of strain. The chief differences between men in such stormy weather are not the differences between those who are in turmoil and those who are not in turmoil, for the latter do not exist, but the differences in their responses to disturbing situations. All experience the storm, but not all experience it in the same way. Though the storm may be beyond our power, the response is not.

An important element in the right conduct of life is the

ability to gauge with accuracy what the precise nature of the present human predicament is. Nothing is gained when we provide answers to questions which people are no longer asking or when we attack non-existent evils. Unless we know the temper of the age, we shall waste most of our effort. It is essential to wisdom about life to recognize which dangers are perennial and which ones are only temporary. Though there is no change in the fundamental human situation, there are striking changes in the ways in which people respond. These changes, being largely the result of passing fashions of thinking, will not, of course, be permanent, but, for the moment, they are of urgent practical importance and must, consequently, be understood. It is clear, to all who try to be sensitive, that something of significance is now occurring in the western world. Some speak of it as a revolution in values, while others diagnose it as a sickness. Possibly it is something of both. One of the most articulate of modern humorists, Malcolm Muggeridge, believes that what we are witnessing is the triumph of a new barbarism. Some readers will remember that Lord Macaulay, writing as early as 1857, predicted the possibility that America could be "laid waste by barbarians in the twentieth century as the Roman Empire was in the fifth." The probability, of course, is that extreme estimates of optimism and despair are both exaggerated and therefore inaccurate. In any case, the barbarism which Macaulay predicted will come, if it does come, from the inside of our culture and not from some external invader.

Whatever it is that is going on around us, it is intimately associated with moral issues. A generation ago it was often asserted that the primary danger to our civilization lay in a lack of moral concern. People seemed to be satisfied with their own affluence, if they could achieve it, and were not, it appeared, deeply concerned about social evils. No thoughtful observer would make such an estimate now. It may be that people are wrongly concerned, or that they are uncritical in their emotional excitement, but there is no doubt about the widespread nature of the concern. Indeed, it is no exaggeration to say that moral questions are almost the only ones which interest modern man. In the colleges there is a discernible movement away from the former concentration upon the natural sciences, with the prospect of a real shortage, eventually, in this field, while the evils of human conduct are discussed endlessly. Far from ours being a generation that can truly be described as amoral, our mistake, if there is one, lies in our actually being hyper-moral. It is difficult to think of another period in recorded history when the concern for social conduct has been more widespread and more intense.

The very intensity of our preoccupation with moral matters may be, in the long run, part of our salvation. When ancient Rome succumbed to the triumph of barbarism, there were some who sensed the danger, but there is no evidence that it was sensed by the masses of the people. If the present popular mood can be guided into the right channels it may, ultimately, provide a basis of hope.

The frequent references to the war in Indo-China as being "an immoral war" provide an accurate disclosure of contemporary mentality. Even those whose opposition is plainly political find it expedient to state their opposition in moral terms. The words on the placards seldom express messages of a political or an economic nature; they are, in the majority of instances, moral pronouncements. Brief as they are, they tell us something important about contemporary human life, as they carry freight of both good news and bad news.

Among the most astute observers of the current scene is Daniel Patrick Moynihan, Counsellor to the President and Professor at Harvard. More succinctly than most, Professor Moynihan has seen the significance of a tendency in which all questions, including the economic and political, are, in our current mentality, reduced to moral terms. His major conclusion on this subject is as follows:

> In a curious, persistent way our problem as a nation arises from a surplus of moral energy. Few peoples have displayed so intense a determination to define the most mundane affairs in terms of the most exalted principles, to see in any difficulty an ethical failing, to deem any success a form of temptation, and as if to ensure the perpetuation of the impulse, to take a painful pleasure in it all. Our great weakness is the habit of reducing the most complex issues to the most simplistic moralisms.

The noisy and violent protests, which mark our age, and to which we are now accustomed, constitute a kind of revelation. Is it not amazing that thousands of people are willing to forsake their ordinary employments for several days, risking or even welcoming arrest, for one primary reason: to affirm a moral judgment? We must remember that concentration upon something conceived to be evil is always the justification of whatever is done in this fashion, including the violence. Even those who hinder innocent and unoffending persons from going to their daily work claim to have a moral justification for their act. Paradoxically, the freedom of others is denied in the name of freedom, while the assertion of civil rights in the abstract may involve the denial of the civil rights in the concrete. This is just one of the many reasons why we need more careful attention, not to temporary moral issues, but to the fundamental questions of what the good life is. We are not concerned merely with survival; man is called, not merely to live, but to live well.

Whatever the truth may be about our time, it is complex. In one sense, Muggeridge is right in his judgment that barbarism has already descended upon civilization. We know this when we hear the chanting and observe the broken windows. It is manifestly barbaric to perpetrate violence, in condemnation of violence. There is an element of barbarism whenever people break the peace in order to affirm their love of peace. It is always barbaric to shout down an opponent, thus refusing to listen to whatever he may say, for the essence of barbarism is the rejection of the life of reason. Barbarism is revealed when phrenetic speech displaces calm and rational inquiry, and when equal consideration to all of the live options is rejected.

We ought to be grateful for the general renewal of moral concern. However confusing and self-contradictory the actions of the popular moralists may be, they at least indicate a recognition of what the nature of the problem is. There is, fortunately, a general understanding to the effect that the problems of mankind are deeper than we have supposed and that the solutions must, accordingly, be deeper than those generally proposed. Problems of urbanization, of pollution, and of noise, are superficial ones, when compared to the fundamental question of how a man ought to live with his neighbors. If we are not clear at the center, there is little probability of our being clear on the edges.

We should try to learn all that we can from the fact that the greatest single concentration of moral judgment is that which appears in colleges and universities. Part of this is the result of the widespread recognition of the inadequacy of mere knowledge. The once widely held notion that education serves, automatically, to make people wise and good is now thoroughly exploded. People in academic communities are not conspicuously more reserved in their judgments, or more fair to one another, or even more honest in their dealings, than are people outside the halls of learning. Sin is no respecter of academic status! Part of the turmoil in our universities arises from the fact that people were once oversold and overpromised about what education would be able to accomplish. The honest recognition of this by contemporary professional educators is like a fresh breeze. One splendid example of such forthrightness comes from an acknowledged educational leader, President Landrum Bolling of Earlham. "More often than we would care to admit," Dr. Bolling has written, "the liberal intellectual community is characterized by attitudes (quickly detected by outsiders) that reveal self-righteousness, overconfidence, and moral arrogance."[1]

Even though the contemporary moralism involves an element of hope, its effectiveness is hindered by the widespread cult of anti-intellectualism. Too often it is assumed that moral judgments are simple and clear, without

[1] *The Earlhamite, Fall,* 1970, p.1.

the need of rigorous analysis. To our sorrow, conventional moralism has become stylized and consequently is received uncritically. Most of the new moralism is directed to the iniquity of four objects of denunciation: war, racial tension, poverty, and pollution, opposition to any of which can elicit instant and enthusiastic support. In short, our age is marked by an excess of moral concern, with a minimum of ethical inquiry. It is very likely that, as historians look back upon our generation, with the benefit of hindsight, they will describe it as the age of "Moralism without Ethics." Our shame is that we assume that we know, and that the issues are simple. In short, we, like the Athenians of the great age of Greece, need terribly the message to the effect that wisdom emerges, in the first instance, in the recognition that we do not know.

Much of our own hope lies in the potential recovery of rationality. We must remember that Socrates, who was himself the victim of an emotional wave of moral denunciation, saw no hope except in clear thinking. His major insight was to the effect that reason can be employed and, in fact, must be employed, if we are to avoid disaster. In several historical periods, this particular insight has been neglected, with consequent disaster.

As we look rationally at the current tendency to discuss all issues in moral terms, we find much that is distressing. The intense moral fervor which is illustrated in nearly all public disputes seems not to carry over into genuine sympathy for individual persons. Thus it is very common for there to be extreme harshness in the judging of national leaders, the greatest harshness being expressed by those who think of themselves as being engaged in some moral crusade. By some curious twist of the modern mind, the maligning of the characters of others does not seem to be inconsistent with the picture of what morality requires.

What is really new is the dominance of an angry mood. Those who are personally angry and who try to whip up anger in others, particularly in the marching mob, tend to lose all perspective. The mood, of course, is enhanced as it is expressed, and most of all, if it is expressed by a group in which the vociferous judgments are mutually reinforcing.

An extremely disturbing factor in the popular moralizing is that it is as unlaughing as it is unloving. There seems to be little opportunity for humor when people are perpetually angry. It is important to note that even the supposedly humorous magazines are now less productive of laughter as they engage, ever more deeply, in moral crusading and in violent denunciation of those with whom they happen to disagree.

The emergence of the mood of unlaughing concern has appeared, not among the oppressed, but among the affluent and the overprivileged. It is among these, rather than among the poor, that there is evidence of the most extreme self-righteousness. Partly out of a sense of guilt for having been the recipients of too much, these crusaders go forth with the utmost grimness to denounce the social order by which they are supported.

One of the chief marks of irrationality in the current moral scene is the separation of social from personal values, which amounts to a denial of integrity. It is almost conventional for representatives of the popular moralism to be deeply concerned about the four public evils mentioned above, but to have absolutely no concern for either personal honesty or marital fidelity. The effort to eliminate public evils singly and together has taken on the character of a religion, the intensity of the faith being measured by the bitterness with which supposed enemies are attacked, in a mood similar to that of the Inquisition. But personal integrity is something else and is, in fact, seldom mentioned.

What is extremely important, and what is easy to miss, is that a divided morality represents only a partial ethics. It stresses, sometimes in a truly committed manner, the side of morality which has to do with public wrongs, but, in its standard expression, it frequently neglects private morality. According to this version, a man in public life is easily forgiven for engaging in adultery, provided he is sufficiently vocal in emphasizing the needs of poor people or the evil of racial discrimination. It is not at all uncommon for protesters against social ills to steal food from public dining rooms or to cheat airlines by some dodge. What is strange is not that people engage in theft, for that has been going on from the beginning of civilization, but rather that personal honesty should be considered unimportant.

Every thoughtful person wishes that the picture of a fragmented though intense moralism were a caricature, but unfortunately it is not. There is in existence an entire sub-culture in which the deliberate fragmentation of ethical conduct, rather than being the exception, is actually the rule. This needs to be understood in contemplating the much publicized sexual revolution. What is new is not that some people are adulterous for that is, indeed, an old story, but rather the fact that there is a new though confused ideology. This is not the ideology of the person with whom we have been familiar, who, refusing to allow any moral factors to inhibit his conduct, simply tries to operate as though moral values do not exist or as though they have no significance in human conduct. What we have on our hands now, by sharp contrast, is something of a radically different character. We are faced with the philosophy of people who are vociferously moral at one point, but who do not see the necessity of wholeness. We must be honest enough to face the fact that we have great numbers in our culture, especially among the supposedly most privileged, who think that they can combine, without contradiction, a burning concern over social wrongs and promiscuity on the level of sexual experience. They do not have a bad conscience about using another human being for the sake of a sexual thrill, simply because they do not think it is wrong to do so. What we are observing is, in some ways, a devaluation of the significance of sex.

A fragmented morality, however intense part of the dedication may be, will lead to inevitable disaster. It is essential to the character of a tragic flaw that it *widens*. A vivid illustration of this is now provided by the voluntary communes which are emerging in various parts of our country. The Utopian fellowships are idealistic in their intense rejection of a materialistic way of life, but marital fidelity is not, in most instances, seen by them as an objective value. The murder trial of Charles Manson and his female associates is significant because the attitudes of the real extremists may show us something which we might otherwise miss. *The meaning of any position is revealed when it is carried to its logical end.* As the moral flaw widens, the probability of eventual disaster approaches certainty.

There are a few tasks more important in our time than the balancing of an emotional moralism by a rational ethics. It is possible, if men are willing to do so, to study the problems of what men ought to do with the same objective rigor that they apply to the study of physics or chemistry. Fortunately, there are few fields of intellectual inquiry in which there are so many acknowledged masterpieces, because of which we are not forced to depend merely upon our own unaided efforts. All who are acquainted with it recognize that the first systematic study of ethics, that of Aristotle, is as helpful to us today as it was to Greek readers in the fourth century B.C. *The Nicomachean Ethics,* as the first systematic statement is called, has contemporary pertinence, in that Plato's famous student set the standard of all subsequent inquiry by his clear warning that the good life is neither easy nor simple. "Men cherish the notion," Aristotle said in Book V of his masterpiece, "that, since it lies in their own power to do a right or wrong thing, it must be easy to be righteous. That is a mistake. It is easy enough to go to bed with your neighbor's wife, or hit the man next to you, or grease the palm of some personage — that sort of thing anyone can do. In like manner it is easy to perform a good action, but not easy to acquire a settled habit of performing such actions."

Aristotle has had many worthy successors, some of whom have lived in the recent past. An outstanding example of greatness in the field of ethical inquiry is *The Methods of Ethics,* by Henry Sidgwick, yet it appears that many who talk glibly of what is moral or immoral have not even bothered to examine a book of this character. We get a fair view of Professor Sidgwick's ethical *opus* when we note what he said of his book in the Preface to the first edition. "It claims," he said, "to be an examination, at once expository and critical, of the different methods of obtaining reasoned conviction as to what ought to be done."

The disciplined study of ethics is a noble enterprise, but it is important to warn the reader not to expect more than can be provided. Aristotle, himself, warned that ethics cannot, in the nature of things, be an exact science. We must, in each science, seek only that degree of exactness which the subject matter in each case allows. It is obvious that we should be foolish to require the same exactness in ethics that can be achieved in physics. Furthermore, it would be false to claim that the study of philosophical ethics necessarily makes men either happy or good. If it did, philosophers would be pre-eminent in these respects, yet the truth is that they often are not. The ablest of philosophers have disclaimed either wisdom or goodness in themselves. Nevertheless, it is true that the more we can study, with intellectual rigor, the most important questions, the better the outcome, for both individuals and society, is likely to be.

There are a few basic moral principles which have been discovered and carefully enunciated and which transcend particular cultural formulation. The first of these is the principle of consistency. It is neither accidental nor trivial that this has been widely recognized as the Golden Rule. It becomes the very touchstone of the scientific examination of morality at the hands of Socrates and gives point to several of the Dialogues of Plato. In the brilliant handling of Immanuel Kant (1724-1804) it came to be known as the Categorical Imperative. The negative form of this imperative, which is the most vivid and memorable, is as follows: *Never make yourself an exception to your own rule.*

If this principle were understood and honored in the modern world it would provide an antidote to a great deal of confusion. For example, any person who tries to exemplify the principle of consistency will certainly not deny to his opponents the right of free expression, while demanding it for himself. If he wants to be listened to, he will listen. But every candid observer is well aware that, in our current malaise, this principle often seems not even to be considered, much less obeyed. Anarchy is obviously a self-contradictory moral philosophy because, if it were universally applied, nothing, not even the promotion of anarchy, could be promoted. The only world in which the anarchist can operate is one in which his own principle is not generally accepted.

A second universal principle of any sound ethics, and one which is often unrecognized, is that of comparative difficulties. The essence of this principle emerges as soon as we transcend *naivete* sufficiently to realize that, in our highly complex world, there are no perfect choices. This is why the simplistic solution is always inadequate. As we face the defense of our country there are obvious difficulties, including the heavy expense involved in maintaining armed forces. But, if we are intellectually honest, we are also bound to recognize that there are enormous difficulties in any system of government which does not have armed forces. The Founding Fathers, keenly conscious of this practical situation, reached the conclusion that the difficulties of the latter position outweighed the difficulties of the former one.

One of the most sophisticated of all ethical truths is the one we reach when we finally realize that the "best" and the "least evil" are identical in denotation. In the human predicament there does not appear to be any option that does not include some elements which are undesirable. In short, it is our lot to live, not in some Utopia, but in the mixture. Evils are involved if I am away from home, but there are other evils, including omission of possible services, if I remain at home. Wisdom lies, not in rejecting a course because it fails to be ideal, but in honest comparison of courses that are practically possible. The best is never the ideal best, for we do not live in an ideal world; it is always the best under the circumstances. There is evil in smoke, but there is also evil in lack of heat for people's houses. The one who is an ethicist and not merely a moralist will try to see which of these is worse. If two options exhaust the possibilities, it is clearly wicked to reject the lesser evil in favor of the greater evil. This is not the way people like to have it, but this is the way it is.

Two influential thinkers have elucidated the conception of comparative evils in our century. They are the late Professor John Baillie, of the University of Edinburgh, and the late Professor H.G. Wood, of the University of Birmingham. Both of these tough minded men taught that one of the chief methods of philosophy is that of balancing imperfect alternatives. What we require, in the cultivation of the good life, is not a simplistic contrast between goods and evils, but the kind of sensitivity which makes us choose one path, not because we like it, but because all known alternatives are worse. Much of the vociferous condemnation of our time would be avoided if this kind of ethical sophistication were achieved or even understood.

There is real hope in the recognition of the fact that men have often been driven to good thoughts in bad times. Because the unexamined life is not worth living, it is important that, in our generation, we try again to make a serious and sustained effort to describe the standard by which our actions are to be judged. What we seek, when we do this, is the triumph of rationality. Rationality, we are well aware, does not insure success in the right conduct of life, but we at least know that *irrationality* insures failure.

Ethics has long been desirable, but now it is necessary. It is the recognition that we live in a moralistic age that drives us to the necessity of ethics. We must practice ethics if we are to be saved from the excesses of emotional moral fervor, which may easily do more harm than good. Ethics, we must remember, proposes to be a science, by which is meant careful intellectual inquiry. Any system of reasoning must rest finally on some proposition or propositions which open-minded people are willing to accept as intrinsically convincing. This is true even of mathematics and logic, for if a person, when shown a demonstrable conclusion, fails or refuses to see it, there is no more that can be done. All our reasoning is an attempt to bring finally to attention something that sensitive persons can accept on its face value. Otherwise we have the absurdity of continual and unending regress. The ultimate sanction is, therefore, self-evidence.

Accordingly, the best thing we can do for a moral ideal is to describe it in such a way that its intrinsic appeal is made to all who will listen and attend. It is our duty to present the picture of the good life in such a manner that men have a chance to see whether they espouse it or not, and to know which ideal they are choosing to serve.

We may remember, in this connection, that Plato, the most influential of all writing moralists, sought to answer the question of what justice is, not primarily by argument, but by a long and carefully articulated presentation of an ordered society. Justice in the abstract might still elude the questioner, but it was apparently Plato's hope that the concrete picture would give something better than a quick or simple answer, in that the ideal presented in *The Republic* would be so intrinsically attractive that it would need no credentials outside itself. This is still our only way. If the following picture of what man ought to do and be does not appeal to sensitive men and women as a picture of something grounded in reality, there is no more that the author can do.

Important and necessary as careful ethical inquiry may be, it can never, in the nature of the case, be reduced to an exact science or to a strict logical system in which precise conclusions follow necessarily from precise premises. The reason for this is that the moral situation is never simple. Every particular situation is, in one sense, unique, and, though the basic principles are unchanging, they always appear in slightly different combinations. We can never, in the matter of conduct, work out a system of foolproof rules, such that we merely look at the rules and then know, infallibly, what is right. This has been understood from the beginning of serious ethical inquiry and was clearly stated by Aristotle in the following words:

> But let this point be first thoroughly understood between us, that all which can be said on moral action must be said in outline, as it were, and not exactly: for as we remarked at the commencement, such reasoning only must be required as the nature of the subject matter admits of, and matters of moral action and expediency have no fixedness any more than matters of health. And if the subject in its general maxims is such, still less in its application to particular cases is exactness attainable: because these fall not under any art or system of rules.[2]

Though the good life cannot be reduced to mere rules which need only to be applied, this does not mean that we are left wholly without a guide. We have a source of enormous strength in the composite ideal which, for at least two millenniums, has been verified by much experience. This is the Classical-Hebrew-Christian ideal which came into the world by a most remarkable combination of historical events and which has since been elaborated by countless concerned persons. This, the basic feature of what we call the West, has always sought to combine, in one system, the rational vision of the Greeks and the moral vision of the Jews. Elements of this have often lain as seeds for long periods and have finally developed after seeming neglect. The combined vision has always been a disturbing one, so far as entrenched privilege has been concerned. Slavery, for example, as Professor Whitehead has shown in *Adventures of Ideas,* was already undermined as soon as this vision was part of our heritage, though it took eighteen hundred years for the implications of the vision to be fully understood and accomplished.

[2]*Nicomachean Ethics*, II, 1104a.

The moral ideal which we supposedly espouse in the life of the West, but which we demonstrate so inadequately and with so little consistency, is not often or easily presented as a unit. Instead it is found in scattered bits, in many books and in many separated ethical systems. What we need now is a bringing together of these scattered parts into a unified whole, so that we may see something of the entire pattern of the life about which we really care. The chapters which follow, since they are written with this aim in mind, are not separated chapters, but are elements in a total picture of what life might be. Only as we see this ideal in its wholeness does it have compelling power on our minds. If once we catch some vision of a life which is good for men, both individually and collectively, then it is our *duty* to make that kind of life prevail. Thus our moral philosophy is based on the conviction that the "ought" depends ultimately on the "good."

It is obvious that there has often been violent disagreement among ethical thinkers, but, in spite of this disagreement, there is an astonishing amount of practical wisdom about living on which agreement has been substantial. The tragedy of the disintegration of so many lives, when human civilization seems otherwise advanced, is not a necessary tragedy, for there is a positive lead to follow and it is truly precious to those who find it. This lead is not the discovery of any one person, but is the combined discovery of many persons through many centuries, often in diverse cultures. It is one of the paradoxes of moral philosophy that, while those who are accounted the experts in this field of inquiry frequently argue tenaciously about the sources of moral insight and about the basis of authority, they are often in substantial agreement on *what is right*. Whatever the differences in theory, the practical agreement is amazing. Indeed this unanimity is part of the evidence for the existence of an objective moral order, independent of ourselves, conformity with which constitutes the truth, insofar as truth can be known by finite beings.

Can we state these agreed principles in language which the modern seeker can understand and to which he may respond? The conviction is that we can and furthermore that we *must*. When we seek to do this, we are engaging in the most practical of human endeavors. There are two practical effects which sound ethical thinking should have. In the first place, it should have a direct bearing on the course of events. A people who really understand what they prize act in ways greatly different from the ways of those who are confused or unconvinced. We must restate the fertile vision in such a way that it may inspire us to dedication and ultimately to action which alters history. In the second place, such thinking ought to help us to have something on which to fasten in the midst of whatever disasters we, as individuals, may have to endure.

Hard as our problem may be, it is no new problem. Man has lived through dark ages before, but survival has not been accidental or natural. Valuable contributions have sometimes emerged from dark ages only because some men, in the midst of the darkness, have made it their main business to keep alive the things that are most precious, without which no enduring order can be constructed. Thus there lived a man named Boethius in Rome, fifteen hundred years ago, after the old Roman order had been shattered and the Dark Age had set in. This man was finally thrown in prison by a despotic government, but, inside the prison, he wrote one of the enduring testaments of the human spirit. This book, *The Consolation of Philosophy*, is a brilliant example of how light can be preserved in the darkness. The experience of the Roman philosopher has a singular appropriateness now, because there is a sense in which we are all in prison. Like Boethius we must seek whatever enduring values there are that are independent of the changing political or military scene. Like him, in the face of adversity, we may be able to catch a sense of the relativity of both our common goods and our common evils. To do this is to achieve a philosophical stance, in which we refuse to exaggerate on either side. If our material fortune seems fleeting, we can be sure that material misfortune will be equally fleeting and that both miss the main point of human life. "For this is sure and this is fixed by everlasting law," said "Philosophy" to the imprisoned Boethius, "that naught which is brought to birth shall constant here abide."

There is something about dark times that may actually lead to more profound thought on the central questions. It is possible for men to be more clear-eyed in disaster than they are in prosperity. It is surely no accident that the noblest literature of the ancient Hebrews was produced during the Babylonian captivity and that the noblest words ever uttered in America came in the darkness of the Civil War. Now, at last, we have the Civil War of the whole world and we require voices to help us to achieve "firmness in the right as God gives us to see the right."

One of the greatest dangers which we face in our confused

time is that a dull despair may settle down over the minds of the majority of the people as it becomes clear that our century is one of continuing strain. That we are in tragic times all interpreters agree, but if the mood of despair becomes general the very effort to change the course of events will cease. We are well aware that, even when we try, we may actually fail, but failure is *certain* if we give up to despair. Since ideas have changed history before, we are justified in the conviction that they may do so again.

II

THE DEMAND FOR MEANING

Life is not lost by dying! Life is lost
Minute by minute, day by dragging day,
In all the thousand, small, uncaring ways.
—STEPHEN VINCENT BENÉT[1]

The life we prize is seriously threatened, not primarily by any probability of attack from a foreign power, but by the battle of ideas within our own Western society. The battle of ideas is the major battle of our time and it is one particularly easy to lose. Without a full realization that we have done so, we may introduce discordant conceptions, which not only destroy harmony, but also diminish our vitality. Sometimes we attempt the impossible, in that we try to combine sets of ideas which are mutually incompatible, and the result is always weakness. Only a consistent picture of life as it ought to be, and as it might be, can catch our imagination so that we face our time with zest. If our picture is unclear, or if we try to hold mutually contradictory ideas, the zest is sure to be lacking.

The lack of zest is one of the most striking features of our age. Recent observers in Peking report from China a mood of terrific expectancy in the revolutionary mentality which makes our dullness and confusion all the more striking by contrast. The enthusiasm of the Chinese may not, of course, continue,

[1] "A Child is Born," from *We Stand United and Other Radio Scripts*, published by Rinehart & Company, Inc. Copyright, 1942, by Stephen Vincent Benét. Reprinted with permission of the publisher.

and we have reason to believe that the system now represented there includes fundamental errors in its very structure, but at the moment the contrast in morale is great and this should be sobering to us. We ought to know that, in the long run, a people with no sense of lift and enthusiasm will be no match for those driven by fanatical devotion to an ideal, no matter how perverted that ideal may be.

What we are now experiencing in the Western World is really a depression, but it is not the depression which has normally been expected, namely, an economic one. For several years various persons have warned that a depression might come, and we have said up to now that the prophets of doom were wrong about this, but actually the prediction has materialized, though in an unexpected way. What we have is a *moral depression*. The stock market is still strong, and the price structure has not broken, but something more serious is happening and will become much worse unless we can take steps to check the movement.

The paradox is that our moral depression has come in the midst of better economic conditions than have been known for many years or perhaps have ever been known anywhere. If economic factors were really the determining factors, as some philosophies hold, this could not be true, but it is. The moral depression has not come in poverty-stricken lands, but in the midst of almost full employment, high wages and abundant food. The contrast between our economic condition and that of the majority of the human race is so great that we can hardly imagine it, though several able writers have recently done their best to make us see it.[2] We understand something of the con-

[2] See Stringfellow Barr, *Let's Join the Human Race*.

trast when we realize that, in Southeast Asia, the people look upon starvation in the same way that *we* look upon cancer; it is deplorable, but, so far, *unavoidable*, and thus a necessary calamity, to be suffered without complaining.

It might be understandable if people faced with starvation should lose their nerve, but there is something seriously wrong when people, living in the midst of plenty, go to pieces by the millions. Yet this is precisely what is occurring in the citadel of democracy. Millions of men and women, with sufficient to eat and to wear, and with no experience of being bombed or made homeless, are actually holding on in desperation, trying not to go to pieces! In many parts of the Western World we are under the constant necessity of increasing our facilities for the care of the mentally ill, but this is not the point at which the situation is most disturbing. Great as is the problem presented by those who require mental hospitalization, this is by no means the most serious problem that we face. Our most serious problem in this area is that presented by the many who are classed as normal, but actually are deeply disturbed. While there are thousands in our advanced society who go to pieces so badly that they must be cared for in public establishments for that purpose, there are many millions outside such institutions whose full usefulness is largely destroyed by constant anxieties and fears.

Our moral depression is a scandal because it shows so strikingly the hollowness of our high pretensions. Our pride in making ingenious things is deprived of all justification if, in making the things, we lose that for which the things are made. A sobering illustration of this paradox of failure in the midst of success is provided by the great city of Detroit, which, in so many ways, stands before us as an exaggerated symbol of modernity. Insofar as ours is an age of the internal combustion engine, Detroit is the key city of the planet. In this city, cars that are truly marvelous productions are turned out with almost incredible speed, but what of the men who make them? We know something important about our age when we know that the local name for the offices of one of the big motor companies is "ulcer alley." The stomach ulcer is one of the chief symptoms of our particular depression. It humbles our pride to face the fact that we who are so clever at making machines are often failures in the more important business of the personal lives, by whom and for whom the machines are made.

We have a fairly accurate index of the numbers of such people in the very popularity of the literature which is advertised as a cure. Books dealing with peace of mind, peace of soul and the recovery of confidence have been among the best sellers for almost a decade and the demand for them is apparently inexhaustible. The relevant consideration here is that, while the popularity of a medicine may not tell much about its efficacy as a cure, it does tell a great deal about the range of occurrence of the disease. The popular books on the achievement of confidence, peace or poise are eloquent testimony to the fact that millions are now conscious of the lack of these very qualities and are desperate in their attempt to secure them. The bookseller's report is therefore pathetic news. We know what people do *not* have when we see what they strive hectically to secure. It is not the happy, but the deeply sad who are preoccupied with the problem of happiness; it is not the well-married who are eager to read all the available books on sex; it is not the whole, but the sick, who seek a physician.

There is no need to multiply evidence of the existence of our moral depression, since that is generally admitted. What is practically more important is to give our best thought to critical analysis of causes and, consequently, to cure. The popular explanation of our trouble is to blame our situation on the pace of our mechanical age, and particularly on the speed of living which seems to be inseparable from an urban society. There is a measure of truth in this claim, but it is very far from the whole truth. Something of the inadequacy of this explanation is shown by the fact that the one state in which a really careful survey of mental illness has been made, and where the incidence has been found to be particularly high, is the state of Kansas, which is one of our least urban areas. Moreover, there are men and women, in the midst of the noise and bustle of a mechanized civilization, who have maintained a sense of life's meaning and are in no danger of going to pieces.

Though modern mechanization is not the sufficient cause of our loss of nerve, it does have two striking effects. In the first place, it *reveals* weaknesses pitilessly and, in the second place, it accentuates, by modern methods of communication, our fears and anxieties. Mechanization provides the ordinary person with more data to worry about than any other generation has ever known.

While the rapidity of the pace of living in a mechanical age undoubtedly contributes to our ills, the lack of an adequate philosophy may contribute to them much more. Some, it is true, read the Great Books, some have deep religious faith, a few have inherited standards and disciplines of behavior, but the majority are essentially uprooted. Our consolations are the dubious consolations of the bored—the daily newspaper, the radio program, the motion picture and television. Unsatisfying as these are, we are often unable to think what else to do with our free time. We rush; we cannot bear to be alone; and we have little acquaintance with the experience of quietness or meditation. A characteristic symbol is that of the nervous commuter, whose time in transit might reasonably be a magnificent opportunity for quiet meditation, but who is obviously restless and who spends the last few minutes of the daily journey standing in the aisle of the train to save seconds in getting off. These people will not be cured by reading a book; their cure will be difficult and it will involve a complete reorientation of their lives. The solution will come in the sphere of convictions and not in any alteration of our mechanical structure or any retreat from it to some scene of preindustrial simplicity.

The habit of war in our century is a contributing factor to our ills, comparable to mechanization. War does not *cause* our depression of spirit, but often reveals it and accentuates it. But we shall not escape war any more than we escape industrialization. The chance that most of us now living will see, in our entire lifetime, anything that can reasonably be called international peace is extremely slight. Peace in our time is as unlikely as was prosperity in the South immediately after the American Civil War, because the conditions of peace simply do not exist, and we cannot see how they may arise for a very long time. There has been so much hatred, and so much justifiable mistrust, that it may be generations before the political and social storms can subside. Certainly we cannot go back to some idyllic situation which some of us dimly remember and of which many nostalgically dream. We must never forget that disturbance has been man's common lot and that, though we have tended to suppose otherwise, peace is the exception. There has never been total peace in the world and the periods of relative calm have been exceptions to the rule.

The way out, for modern man, is to learn to live well, not apart from the strain but *in it*. Our line of advance is not away from the storm, but through it, in the mood of the men who have flown the North Atlantic so successfully every day for the past ten years. What we require is not a formula for peace, which, humanly speaking, is impossible, but rather *a formula for living wisely and well in the midst of continuous strain.*

There was a popular formula which was ably expressed and widely believed in the confused period of apparent peace from 1946 to 1950. This formula began with the major premise that peace of mind was the supreme human good, and then proceeded to show how this boon could be achieved. The essential message of the secular and religious books on this subject was the same, though the emphasis sometimes differed in that the secular volumes were handbooks on the art of happiness while the religious ones presented faith as instrumentally valuable in the overcoming of anxiety. Any reader who has watched sermon titles, as found on church bulletin boards or on the church page of the Saturday newspaper, will understand what is meant. Insofar as this preaching, whether secular or clerical, has been effective in helping distraught men and women to overcome frustrations and live useful lives, we must be everlastingly grateful, but the emphasis now seems to be severely dated. We have come into a sterner time, when a sterner message is required. There is a great and neglected message, so curiously avoided in the recent past, in the words of Jesus,

"Do not think that I have come to bring peace on earth; I have not come to bring peace, but a sword."

Joshua Liebman's *Peace of Mind*, coming as it did in 1946, near the beginning of our short and delusive peace, must be looked upon, not so much as a book, as a historical event. The enormous success of this volume and of the many similar ones which followed it, tells us a great deal about our age and its popular mentality. That individual readers were helped by reading these books, we cannot doubt, but that is not the relevant consideration now. If we see the success of books like Liebman's as an insight into our age, we learn what men and women have believed in the midst of their confusion and we learn, at the same time, some of the causes of our present predicament.

Blasphemous as it may sound to our generation, peace of mind is not the ultimate ideal in the life of the individual. The reason for this is that peace is possible on many levels. There is the peace of the man like Boethius in prison, or Socrates drinking the poison, but there is also the peace of the self-righteous man who, having felt justified in all his acts, has a singularly "untroubled mind"; he has an easy conscience because he is sure of his virtue. In his important novel, *The Fountain*, Charles Morgan makes one of his characters say of another, "Lapham has peace of mind when he's had a good dinner and his pipe is drawing."

It is surely not self-evident that the experience of the artist or the saint, marked, as it so often is, by a restless urge for something better, is really less valuable than is the experience of the person who is at peace because he is satisfied with his mediocrity. If peace of mind is really what we seek, then we cannot avoid the logical conclusion that the life of the complacent person is better, but to accept this is to go against the judgment of the most sensitive of our race in many generations.

We ordinarily think of peace of mind as the serenity of a saint or the courage of a Stoic slave like Epictetus, but this is only one variety. Before we know whether peace of mind is an unconditional good, we need to know a great deal else. In fact, there are many conditions under which a man *ought not* to have peace of mind and under which a good man *will not* have it. There are many situations in which a man ought to be severely disturbed or shaken. There are times, even according to the teachings of the New Testament, when men ought to be angry, and there are countless times when they ought to be aroused.

There is, undoubtedly, an ultimate peace, a center of calm even in the midst of storm, and for this we must strive, but we are utterly mistaken about the human situation if we suppose that this goal involves complacency in the face of injustice or easy tolerance of wanton cruelty. The deeper peace we may ultimately achieve is wholly compatible with disturbance at another level, but the mistake so many have made is that of supposing that the level of disturbance can be avoided. The deeper peace comes only by great difficulty and through much pain. If peace is reached too cheaply it turns out to be spurious.

Our very concern for personal happiness is really one of the chief symptoms of our moral disease. It may seem curious to speak of happiness as a problem but a problem it is. The problem begins to appear when we make the double observation that all men desire happiness and that the direct search for happiness is somehow debasing. It is obvious that men would rather be happy than sad, if faced with a simple choice, but, at the same time, we are forced to admit that most of those whom we honor in human history have been strangely uninterested in the question whether they were personally happy. Our heroes are men and women who have cared about justice or truth and have not even raised the happiness question at all. *Actually* of course, many of them have been gloriously happy, but it is not happiness at which they have aimed.

This observation is part of what has long been known as the hedonistic paradox, to the effect that happiness is lost if it is the direct aim of a person's life, whereas it often comes abundantly, provided it is neglected. *To get happiness you must forget it.* We have an interesting manifestation of this paradox in the mood of our own day in that the popular guidebooks to happiness, however much they may be read, are not really honored. The average reader may not make a full analysis of the situation, but he understands somehow that this is not the right approach. Something of the revulsion is expressed by the credo in the first issue of *The New American Mercury*, which declares open opposition to what it calls the "Cult of the Happy" and claims that we have a paper shortage, "because of all the books telling folks how to Get Happy." Accordingly, *The New American Mercury* is opposed to Happiness, because, say the editors, "the happiest creatures in the world are pigs lying in a wallow."

The hedonistic paradox does not stand alone, but is part of the accumulated ethical wisdom to the effect that concern for self poisons all situations and is ultimately self-defeating. Happiness eludes those who make it their supreme goal, because

there is an element of self-seeking, even in this supposedly noble
search. The difficulty arises in that the elements of the disease
(in this case, concern with self) reappear conspicuously in the
cure. Often the supposed cure is really little more than another
form of the original complaint.

The man who tries to be a vibrant, alert and successful
person, and who reads books on this subject, which claim to
provide him with the appropriate formula, may actually develop some of these characteristics, but this does not mean that
his chief problems are thereby solved. He cannot escape the
consequences of the fact that he is concentrating upon his own
self-interest and self-development. *He has his reward.*

The same principle applies even in the search for humility.
Those who try consciously to be humble frequently end by
demonstrating an especially revolting form of spiritual pride.
Conscious humility is a contradiction in terms, since the adjec-
tive cancels out the noun. Actually much of what is called
humility is only a kind of inverted egocentricity and is worse
than ordinary boastfulness because it includes self-righteousness
as well.

> Once in a saintly passion
>   I cried with desperate grief
> O, Lord, my heart is black with guile
>   Of sinners I am chief.
> Then stooped my guardian angel
>   And whispered from behind
> "Vanity my little man,
>   You're nothing of the kind."[3]

True humility is not thinking badly of oneself, which is only

[3] Unidentified. From T. E. Jessup, *Law and Love* (London: The
Epworth Press), p. 17.

another form of attention to self; true humility is not thinking of oneself at all.

The realization that happiness does not come by seeking is not the end of the matter. Though we live most of our days in what Thoreau so aptly termed "quiet desperation," the average person has had at least a few times when life has seemed worthwhile. There must be conditions under which the good life occurs and other conditions under which it does not occur. Our task is to learn what these are. The path of wisdom is to understand, if possible, the precise nature of the life we really prize and to order our lives accordingly, insofar as that lies within our power. Why do some men sing in prison while others spend their time in self-pity, even in the midst of opulence, physical ease and freedom from external restraints? Why is the slave sometimes more fortunate than his master? Why, with almost identical environment, is one man full of zest while another is frustrated and sad? It has often been noted that those who pay attention to their own aches and pains usually become more ill, while the most fortunate of men and women are those so devoted to a task that no time is left for them to inquire into their blood pressure, or the state of their hearts. This observation is one of many in which we are reminded that real welfare seems to be largely independent of outward circumstances. The good life arises, not primarily from any external factors, but by the inner arrangement, by the mind set, by the attitude. There may be conditions of torture so terrible that man is broken by them, but it is part of the glorious truth about human life that we have a noble tradition of moral freedom within prison walls. Thus George Brockmann, who was a prisoner of the Nazis in Norway during the war, tells of his surprised realization that he was happy in prison. "I was amazed," he said, "to discover, during the fearful misfortune that overwhelmed my country and people during the German occupation, that I had become what they call a happy man."

If a person does not have a source of inner well-being all the pleasures go sour. Witness the frequent sadness of the very rich or even of those with great bodily beauty. The actors in Hollywood are undoubtedly, as a class, far better looking than the average populace, but it is not easily noticeable that their lives are conspicuously enviable for that reason. On the other hand, quite plain people may, because of some purpose in their lives, have an expression which transmutes their physical features. No man in his senses ever suggests that *things* are unimportant, but every thoughtful person knows that the only value of things is their instrumental value, and that they become blessings or curses wholly according to their use, since they have no power of themselves. It is silly to suggest that money is unimportant, because it can be a means of untold good, but it is equally silly to suppose that the mere possession of money brings any person a good life.

What happens to the prisoner or to the invalid or to any person caught in circumstances which he cannot change is potentially twofold. First, he may find some purpose which is so much bigger than he that, in the fight for it, he forgets himself. Second, and consequently, he sees how truly secondary are the many other aims such as money and social standing, which, in less demanding situations, he normally pursues. This apparently is what happens in wartime. Evil and horrible as war is, there is no doubt that it brings tremendous zest and even mental health to multitudes whose lives normally have no element of victory in them. In the pain of all, they tend to forget their own tiny problems and, in the excitement of the total struggle, each life is lifted temporarily to a higher plane. It is part of the shame of our civilization that we have seldom or perhaps never been able to provide a similar situation for the rank and file in time of peace. Our civilization is condemned by the fact that millions really welcome war though they might deny it with their lips. In the motion picture, *The Best Years of Our Lives*, the saddest feature is the title, and particularly the realization of its accuracy.

The reason that millions actually welcome war, whatever they may say, is that war gives significance to little lives. In wartime the work of the farmer, of the mechanic and of so many others suddenly takes on significance because each job seems necessary for final victory. This tells us something very important about human life and something which must be considered in the development of any lasting social or economic system. *Man can bear great physical or spiritual hardship, but what he cannot bear is the sense of meaninglessness.* We must find some way in which our lives count, in which they seem important, or we go mad. The ultimate enemy is not pain or disease or physical hardship, evil as these may be, but *triviality.* What is terrible for men and women is the conviction that they are not needed, that they contribute nothing, and that their lives add up to no enduring meaning.

Most of us, as we think of our own lives, realize that we do not really fear death for ourselves, even though we may fear death for those for whom we care. We know that there are many situations in which death would not be tragic and that there are numerous causes for which we would gladly lay down our little lives, if death should prove to be the necessary price of what we truly value. It is not hard to understand Saint Exupéry, who, shortly before his death, wrote to a friend, "I do not mind being killed in war. . . . As for material things I don't care a damn if they survive or not. What I value is a certain arrangement of these things." What is really tragic is not death for a reason, but the slow petering out of life in self-indulgence, directing the labor of others not to some high end, but to our own bodily comfort. Life that goes out that way, as Benét reminds us in our chapter head quotation, is really *lost*.

If a man begins each day as just another unit of time in which he wonders what to do with himself, he is already as good as dead. The man who really lives always has vastly more to do than he can accomplish and for such a man retirement is almost without significance. How can a man retire from the effort which he believes is sorely needed and which is directed to a really grand cause? It was characteristic of that wonderfully fortunate man, Rufus Jones, the Quaker philosopher, that, though he was eighty-five when he died, he corrected the proof of his last book on the day of his death. It is hardly surprising that he lived in this way if we listen to his teacher, William James:

Whenever a process of life communicates an eagerness to him who lives it, there the life becomes truly significant. . . . But, whenever it is found, there is the zest, the tingle, the excitement of reality; and there is importance in the only real and positive sense in which importance ever anywhere can be.

But how does the zest, which gives the sense of importance, come? How did William James find it? We have already seen that it never comes by concentration on ourselves, our ills, our slights and our *amour-propre*. We are not very important and we cannot really convince ourselves that we are, even were it desirable to do so. We know better. The truth is that we gain a sense of importance for our lives by losing them, and we lose them by devoting them to some ideal, particularly an ideal embodied in a concrete cause. Not all causes are of equal value, by any means, but, psychologically, a poor cause is better than none.

We face at this point a paradox in moral philosophy which demands careful attention if confusion is to be avoided. It is true that happiness comes from within, but it is equally true that the greatest *unhappiness* also comes from within; it comes from focusing attention upon ourselves. In one sense our inner life is our hope, but in another sense our inner life is our terrible danger. The problem is resolved if we realize that the beneficent inner secret is that by which we learn to direct all our major attention and interest to something outside ourselves. Only the unified life brings true well-being, but the unity must be *directional* rather than substantive.

Each one of us is the scene of turmoil, with all kinds of competing motives, ambitions, emotions and desires. Many of our desires are in direct conflict with one another and thus every person is, at some time, a scene of civil war. There is a sense in which each individual is the complex monster of which Plato wrote in *The Republic*.

Whatever else about us is true, we may be sure that we cannot unify our divided and distracted lives from the *inside*. There is little point in the advice that we should follow our natural desires because these desires are so numerous and because, furthermore, many of them are mutually incompatible. There is a natural desire to be boastful and there is also a natural desire to have the approbation of our fellows, but it is very hard to satisfy both of these desires at once, since they cancel one another. As long as we try to unify our lives from within we fail, for again we reintroduce the disease into the supposed cure.

The only way in which a person may achieve relative unity of life is by dedication to something outside himself, to which he gives such loyal devotion that the self is forgotten in the process. The competing parts of our lives, which cannot unite of themselves, are then united because of a unity of direction, when all parts point one way. *The ancient truth is that the health of the self comes, not by concentrating on self, but, by such dedication to something outside the self, that self is thereby forgotten.*

For most men and women there is only one possibility of escape from the bondage of self and that is by the path of loyalty. The object of loyalty may be a cause, another person, an ideal or an institution, but all have the same effect. In each case the pattern is that of the dedication of self to an object about which the individual cares so greatly that he thereby forgets his own pains and frustrations. Full absorption in a cause can even absolve men from the bondage of overwhelming ambition, since the real interest is in the cause and not in proving one's own superiority to others. Ambition, when it is not thus transcended by loyalty, becomes a dangerous element, because so many men take the easy way of proving their superiority by defaming somebody or something else, but genuine loyalty can transcend and transmute personal ambition.

Though we cannot find peace of mind by reading a book about it or by seeking it directly, we may really achieve it if we throw ourselves into the building of a family, a college or a better government. It is true that we cannot find happiness by seeking it, but if we learn to play a violin or write a book or improve a run-down farm, we may wake up someday to realize that we have been wonderfully happy, even in the midst of our inevitable struggles and frequent disappointments. Our self-consciousness, which is a necessary factor in the capacity to make moral judgments, and without which man would not even *be* man, becomes frequently a curse and can be a blessing only when it is lost in the flair for objectivity. The man who becomes so objective that he wishes for the success of a cause or the welfare of another individual, *irrespective of his own contribution to such an end,* has already found salvation from preoccupation with self.

The famous Harvard professor, Josiah Royce, made the fullest statement of this philosophy in a volume which has curiously little influence today, though the central thesis is as applicable to our situation as it was when it was first published more than forty years ago. The volume is entitled *The Philosophy of Loyalty* and represents the final phase of Royce's thought. "There is only one way to be an ethical individual," he wrote; "that is to choose your cause and then to serve it."[4] Loyalty appealed to Royce as a saving power, partly because it was thoroughly democratic in its applicability. "We are not speaking," he said, "of a good that can come to a few men only . . . to heroes or to saints of an especially exalted mental

[4] *The Philosophy of Loyalty* (New York: The Macmillan Company, 1908), p. 98.

type. . . . The mightiest and the humblest members of any social order can be morally equal in the exemplification of loyalty."[5]

Man is such a creature that he needs to *belong*. It is true, of course, that the individual is unutterably precious, that the *one* always counts and that we dare never allow ourselves to think of men and women as expendable units in the mass or mere instruments for the welfare of the state. Man is debased whenever he is seen as merely instrumental, only a means to another's end or even to the end of the entire society, but we must never let this valuable truth hide from us the correlative truth that man is a creature with a need for *membership*. It is no accident that "member," with its implication of organic relations between persons in a society, should have become one of the most used and honored words in our vocabulary, not only in its original religious connotation but in a host of secular situations as well.

We have one of the conditions of the good life when we can function as individuals, and yet individuals who lose themselves, along with other individuals, in some organic whole. This transcends both sheer individualism, with its lonely self-centeredness, and also mass-mindedness. Man reaches the fullness of self only when he finds something to live *for*; he is made that way. However simple this philosophy may seem, it is really profound. When we belong to a cause and give ourselves to it, without counting the cost, our lives achieve both social solidarity and a sense of purpose, which together give significance even to our littleness.

We must face frankly the embarrassing fact that evil causes

[5] *Ibid.*, p. 112.

often have a good effect on the lives of persons devoted to them. Conspicuous modern examples are found among both Nazis and Communists. Nearly all now admit that Hitler's cause was terribly evil, bringing to the world untold harm which has gone on continuously since the final scene underneath the Berlin Chancellory and will go on for decades, but it also is a fact that young men and women of Germany were frequently galvanized into new persons by this movement ten or twelve years ago. They were changed from listlessness to zest; they had something to live for; they had something they were willing to die for. Because these people did not realize that their cause was an evil or inadequate one, and because they were unreservedly committed to it, they were unified at least temporarily.

This means that the philosophy of loyalty, while undeniably true, must be examined critically as we ask the crucial question, "Which loyalty?" It was to this question that Josiah Royce gave his best thought in his famous volume and to which we must give added thought today. Professor Royce's conclusion was that our ultimate safeguard is what he called "loyalty to loyalty." That is, we must ask of our cause whether it is the kind of cause which encourages the maximum loyalty in others or whether it is destructive of other loyalties. "If loyalty is a supreme good," wrote Royce, "the mutually destructive conflict of loyalties is in general a supreme evil."[6] It is worse to rob men of their causes than to maim their bodies, for it is by their causes that they really live. By this standard a loyalty to the Nazi system or a class revolution stands condemned, whereas those who are giving their nights and days to the

[6] *Ibid.*, p. 116.

honoring of the rule of law all over the earth are justified, since their cause is one which, logically, can be universalized.

The best cause is that cause which harms no other and which is big enough to require, and consequently unite, all of our powers. Of course it is a counsel of perfection to tell men to find causes which harm no other, since it is a fact that most causes actually conflict at some points, but it is good to have the ideal clear. It is not enough that a cause should be good for me, uniting my powers by concentrating them on something outside me; it must also be good for others. "And so," concludes Royce, "a cause is good, not only for me, but for mankind, insofar as it is essentially a *loyalty to loyalty*, that is, is an aid and furtherance of loyalty in my fellows."[7] The advice which this philosophy gives to all who are willing to listen, then, is this, "Insofar as it lies on your power, so choose your cause and so serve it, that, by reason of your choice and of your service there shall be more loyalty in the world rather than less. And, in fact, so choose and so serve your individual cause as to secure thereby the greatest possible increase of loyalty among men."[8] To some this may seem too vague, as it perhaps is, but it undoubtedly provides us with a valid general conception. Our task, then, is to proceed, as we are trying to do in the chapters which follow this one, to make the goal more precise. It is to this end that the book has been written.

Psychologically an evil cause may be quite as valuable as a good one, but, if we are concerned with what is right, rather than with what is psychologically successful, we affirm that the adequate object of loyalty can never be a particular nation,

[7] *Ibid.*, p. 118.
[8] *Ibid.*, p. 121.

a particular denomination or a particular class. It is the task of each man who seeks wholeness of life to discover a cause which is universal in its sympathies, even though it works through small units. What we need are small and manageable handles to great designs. Usually such handles are found most satisfactorily by joining ourselves to a movement in which we are conscious that we are in a long succession of men and women who are our partners in the enterprise. What is most rewarding is doing something that really matters with congenial colleagues who share with us the firm conviction that it needs to be done. Few joys are greater than the joy of participation in a dedicated group, and this is a boon which we ought to covet for all men and women. The fact that we join as recruits in a modest part of the total human enterprise does not forfeit the sense of meaning, provided we can see that it is contributory to an ultimate goal. We enter a procession; we are surrounded by a crowd of witnesses; and suddenly we are raised in stature by being an organic part of something bigger than ourselves. We inherit, share and augment a tradition. Being creatures, part of whose potential dignity consists in a keen time sense, we find our true life by entering into a community of memory and of hope.

Saint Exupéry developed brilliantly, in his final phase, the idea that man's life achieves meaning as it cheats the limitations of time. It is man's glory to *dwell*, to make a home, to build an order that can go after his little life is snuffed out. "This I have learned, which is essential," he wrote, "that it behooves us to begin by building the ship and equipping the caravan and erecting the temple which outlasts men."

Man is so made that he cannot find genuine satisfaction

unless his life is transcendent in at least two ways. It must transcend his own ego in that he cares more for a cause than for his own existence, and it must transcend his own brief time in that he builds for the time when he is gone and thereby denies mortality. A man has made at least a start on discovering the meaning of human life when he plants shade trees under which he knows full well he will never sit.

III

THE ACCEPTANCE OF RESPONSIBILITY

Your business is not to clear your conscience
But to learn how to bear the burden on your conscience.
—T. S. ELIOT[1]

The continued and increasing strain under which life must be
lived in our time is essentially the same for all, but the reactions
of different persons to it differ radically. It appears that the
most common reaction is that of some form of escape, and
especially the effort to escape responsibility. Times are bad;
indeed they are so bad and the problems so enormous, that the
individual feels utterly helpless; there seems to be no place
where he can take hold with any effectiveness. In that case, he
argues, he might as well save his energy. Moreover, the care of
great matters is the responsibility of our public men; that is
what we elect them for.

In this disheartening situation the average citizen develops
what may accurately be termed an interim mentality. Since,
emotionally, if not intellectually, we are a people waiting for
a catastrophe, which many think is inevitable, we come to have
the habit of temporary living. This mentality is often an unconscious assumption rather than an explicit affirmation, but it
is not, for that reason, any less effective on general conduct.

[1] *The Cocktail Party*, published by Harcourt, Brace & Co., Inc., New
York, and Faber and Faber, London. Reprinted with permission of the
publishers.

Life is perplexing and anxieties many, so we try to solve the problem by the simple process of running away. Our motto, not only for the young, but for all ages, has become, "Eat, drink and be merry for tomorrow you're drafted." Why, asks the professional student, should I go on with an arduous training when, within a short time, I'll be cannon fodder? Why not have my fling while I can? Why, asks the young woman, should I wait for respectable marriage, when the man I love may never return?

So important in our cultural life is the effort to escape, that great sections of our entertainment are devoted to the process. A measure of the widespread character of the tendency is the degree to which such entertainment has become big business. Some seek escape by reading detective stories, others by constant listening to sentimental broadcasts, others by habitual attendance at the motion picture theaters, and still others by the devoted attention to television programs, which may turn out to be the most effective moral sedative of all. No doubt men have always had a tendency to escape, particularly in difficult times, but never before was it made so easy or were so many attractive facilities provided for the purpose. The owners of the night clubs and the motion picture houses profit greatly by the failure of men and women to find a meaning in their lives, since, as is generally known, a people who have a sense of meaning feel no conscious need of constantly being entertained or amused. Owners of institutions belonging solely to what is fatuously called the entertainment world are like the managers of undertaking parlors; they gain personally by what is tragedy for others.

Though alcoholism is the most obvious means of escape from

insignificance, it is now well understood that this weakness does not stand alone; it is, instead, merely one extreme form of a distressingly common process, the process according to which men and women try desperately to center their attention on something which will, at least temporarily, make them forget the vacuity of their own lives. A revealing fact is that, in Great Britain, drunkenness has been lessened with the growing popularity of the motion pictures. In short, one form of escape makes another unnecessary, since all conform to the same general pattern.

Revealing as are the modern ways of escape expressed in actions, they are not nearly as revealing as are the ways of escape expressed in ideas. While we give lip service to the Judeo-Christian heritage, and while this complex of ideas affects some of our practice, we have, in great measure, adopted a new orthodoxy which is a watered down version of our radical heritage. We have, in our new orthodoxy of the West, developed a set of axioms which millions of our people accept uncritically without serious examination, on the assumption that they are self-evident. The unifying feature of these popular axioms is that they have the effect of minimizing any serious sense of responsibility. Among these many axioms of modern Western man, three are especially significant:

1. Since God forgives us anyway, it makes little difference how we live.
2. Tolerance is the primary virtue. We must be tolerant of everything because there is always a reason for everything.
3. Because all morality is relative one moral standard is just as good as another.

These axioms combine successfully to give a sense of comfort to those who have been taught that a conviction of guilt is debilitating and therefore something to be avoided at all costs. The easiest way to avoid a guilt complex is to accept a philosophy according to which no act is ever really wrong, and this conclusion is a necessary one if the axioms stated above are accepted as true. We must never, according to our now popular American faith, make a moral judgment on another person, whether he be a murderer in a tavern or a government official who solicits bribes. All that is required, according to the new convention, is to find *why* an act is done and then moral judgment is rendered superfluous.

The doctrine that tolerance is the prime virtue has arisen in supposed emancipation from Puritanical ideas, especially in regard to sexual conduct, but, if it is true, it must, in strict consistency, be applied to all human actions in all situations. If the adage that to understand all is to forgive all, as so many now uncritically believe, is really a sound one and not merely sentimental nonsense, this must be applied to the Marxist plotting the downfall of our way of life, to the Nazi murdering the Jews of Germany or Poland, to the kidnapper who, for the sake of a ransom, puts a damaging fear in the hearts of innocent children for years, and to the pervert who murders a child for the thrill. The doctrine, often influencing judgment as a suppressed premise rather than explicit statement, is that explanation of *causes* is a sufficient approach to a human situation. You don't *blame* a germ; you merely trace its history. Why not do the same with a man? One man is a thief because of the way his early life was conditioned and another man is self-sacrificing for a similar reason. Hitler was what he was, according to this doctrine, because of his formative experiences in Austria. His antisemitism was the result of his bitter experiences after the end of the first World War and, given the conditions, the result came inevitably. *Therefore we should not judge.*

Extreme as this may sound, it is not a caricature of the current doctrine. Of course many will not go this far, but that is merely their failure to follow an idea to its consequences with logical rigor. That what has been presented is not a caricature is shown by the fact that the new intellectual fashion has already made a great difference in the decisions of the common men and women who make up juries for criminal trials. Some juries, in recent trials, where the testimony of psychiatrists has been of primary importance, have obviously worked on the basis of the doctrine mentioned. The juries, we have reason to believe, did not doubt, in some cases, that murder had been committed; what they doubted was the *moral responsibility* of the accused persons. The judgment rendered in such a case is not, therefore, a judgment of fact, but a *value judgment*. If we were to carry this tendency to its logical conclusion we might eventually, as one judge has warned, have nothing but psychiatric reports, and eliminate the judge entirely.

Though the elements of this tendency to produce the easy conscience by emphasis on explanation have long been known in Western society, the tendency has been given a great boost in popular esteem by the wide dissemination of the idea that the different moral codes upheld by different societies show, supposedly, that there is no objective moral standard and also by the general belief that the doctrine of the easy conscience has the support of the *new psychology*, particularly that which stems from the influence of the late Sigmund Freud. It is obvious that this whole situation requires some analysis, if we are to do any straight thinking on a subject so important to our common life. To follow the necessary reasoning is not altogether easy, but the reader may be assured that a great effort has been made to present the necessary steps in the clearest possible way.

It must be said that the tendency to condone all actions, however confused it may be, arises in part from noble motives. It has always been recognized that no person is to blame for that which he cannot help. If murder is committed during a fit of insanity caused by a glandular disturbance, there is manifestly no possibility of moral judgment, because the situation is not a moral situation at all. "Man's will is called *animal*, if necessitated pathologically," says Kant, and in this we must all agree with him.

There are situations which make us very tender in our judgments of others and ought to make us tender, particularly when those called offenders have been reared in extreme poverty or unfortunate home surroundings, but this consideration, important as it is, is by no means the only one which we must keep in mind. It is presumably useful, in facing every human problem, to know all of the past that we can know. There is no good reason why there should not be a psychiatrist at every trial, and we must be glad for whatever such an expert can reveal. But it is illogical in the extreme to suppose, as we often appear to do, that a question of one type eliminates the relevance of a question of another type. It is one thing to know *why* I uttered a derogatory remark about my neighbor, but that does not end a rational inquiry. Perhaps I uttered it because I was angry or because I was envious. Very well; but there remains the question whether I *ought* to have uttered it, and the probability is that I ought *not*, whatever the degree of provocation, or whatever the psychological explanation. Therefore I can condemn my own act, not because I do not understand it, but because I *do*. It may require a certain sophistication to understand the difference between a psychological question and an ethical question, and to realize that intelligent answers to them require different intellectual disciplines, but we ought to be able to reach that level of understanding by now.

The great danger in the emphasis on explanation as sufficient is not in the fact that it tends to make us sentimental about the deeds of others, but that it makes us feel a spurious peace of mind about our own actions. It is obvious that the doctrine that explanation by psychological factors renders moral judgment meaningless applies to ourselves as well as to others. According to this highly comforting notion, each one of us can escape responsibility for whatever he does or fails to do. If I have done an apparently shameful act, the easy answer is, "I was forced to do it by the combination of influences which have made me what I am, and which are wholly beyond my control." If it is escape from the burdensome sense of shame and guilt that we seek, here is the perfect solution of our problem! If the easy conscience, produced by self-tolerance, is a valid conclusion of all analysis, we can be rid forever, not only of the burdening feeling of guilt, but also of the agony of decision. If this is sound philosophy, no one need ever condemn his own action or ask forgiveness. This is the direct road to a certain kind of mental peace, even though it might destroy our entire civilization if it were to become universal in application. But is the conclusion a valid one?

What is required in current thinking is a wholesome skepticism, which involves a rejection of the facile simplification which has been so understandably popular. When we become more realistic and less sentimental we admit that questions which go beyond psychology into the field of ethics are really inescapable ones. This truth sometimes comes home to those who have supposed, in their naïveté, that they could omit such considerations from their lives. They may, indeed, be wholly unconscious of any sense of guilt, partly because they have accepted uncritically the comfortable teaching that a sense of guilt is an abnormality from which they must be liberated, but it is these people who, like the characters in *The Cocktail Party*, are now so confused. The panacea did not work! The good life has not come by the simple expedient of eliminating duty from the vocabulary and this is especially evident as the world storm grows more ominous.

When we begin to examine the intellectual foundations on which the doctrine of the easy conscience is supposed to rest, they turn out to be surprisingly insubstantial. Consider, for example, the presumed scientific basis. There are, apparently, millions in our modern world who may have some common-sense misgivings about the idea that the sense of moral responsibility is now outmoded, but accept it reluctantly because they believe that it is necessitated by the basic principles of science.

The Russians, who hold this view most strongly in their official philosophy, maintain that their position is simply *scientific* and that the rest of the world is still living, in this regard at least, in the prescientific age. The argument is that all events are caused and that the scientific procedure is merely that of finding the conditions. When a rain cloud drops what, to us, is an inconvenient amount of water, the scientist does not judge, condemn or denounce the cloud; he merely shows what the prior atmospheric conditions were which made this action inevitable. Likewise with the botanist. He does not talk about good trees and bad trees; instead he shows how growth can be predicted and altered by planning. The scientific approach to human life, so the argument runs, is to find the causes of human behavior and alter behavior by planning, just as in the case of rain making or in the growth of trees. The Russian intellectuals believe that this is the truth about human life and, unfortunately, a good many in the Western World seem to agree with them. It was the Russian scientist, Pavlov, who popularized the concept of the conditioned reflex, but many Western persons have taken it over as the one supremely scientific approach to an understanding of human behavior. A number of American textbooks teach the adequacy of this conception while many others teach it implicitly.

This general approach to problems has a certain attractiveness, both because of its essential simplicity and also because it seems to be supported by the prestige of science. The conception, however, is far more a matter of philosophy than of science and is not a valid one unless complete determinism is true. But *if* complete determinism is true the very idea of planning, so dear to the hearts of all dialectical materialists, is, by that fact, itself undermined. The botanist may reasonably be supposed to plan the growth of the tree, since his personal decision is outside the system to which the tree belongs, but the whole logical situation is altered radically once the deterministic system is applied to human thought and actions, including moral actions. The social worker likes this philosophy because in terms of it, he can plan a project, perhaps one of slum clearance, and his belief in a deterministic system gives him assurance that his experiment will work effectively in changing human life. Since actions follow inevitably from *prior* physical and social conditions, all he needs to do, according to the theory, is to arrange the conditions and wait for the results.

But the paradox which the planner must face, if he is intellectually honest, *is that in the terms of his philosophy his very effort to plan was itself also determined by prior conditions*. Therefore he does not actually plan at all, but is merely the helpless and passive performer of deeds which are materially necessitated. But this is to destroy, not only any meaning of right and wrong, since the kidnapper and the hero, in such a system, both do what they must; it also destroys any meaning of true and false, since one conclusion is as much necessitated as another. Each believes what he must and that is the end of the matter. But such a conclusion undermines the doctrine as taught, for it is at least claimed by its upholders that it is true. The doctrine in question undermines the whole of rational experience and, therefore, incidentally, undermines itself. If it is true that all acts are necessitated by prior conditions, there is no logical difference between a man deciding to sacrifice his life for a cause and a cloud being blown by the wind. Each does what it *must* do. But, if this is true of human actions, there is no freedom whatever, and we are forced to accept the conclusion that every human thought, including this one, is absolutely necessitated. Why, then, is the denial of freedom more valid than its affirmation? A doctrine which leads to fantastic conclusions is itself suspect.

If any person wishes to maintain this philosophy, he is permitted to do so, but we at least have a right to expect him to be consistent in following his own doctrine. It is notorious, however, that the upholders of the doctrine are not consistent in this matter, as the moralizing of Jacob Malik at Lake Success so vividly demonstrates. By their principle, both praise and blame are meaningless, yet the adherents take credit for accepting their supposedly enlightened principle and condemn others for failure to accept it. Abundant illustrations of such condemnation, when the logic of their own position makes it meaningless, are provided by determinists of both the Marxian and non-Marxian variety.

Though a superficial understanding of science often causes men to arrive at the hasty conclusion that science has no connection with moral judgments, this conclusion is not sustained by careful analysis. It is true that the scientific question is not the same as the ethical question, in that "Why did I do it?" is radically different from "Should I have done it?" but the scientific question is not even possible except upon an ethical basis. Science cannot be divorced from ethics, because science would not be permanently possible except upon a prior basis of trustworthiness. If we should ever give up the basic moral position, according to which a man is strict with himself, even when he might not be detected, in reporting negative evidence as carefully as he reports evidence which supports his favorite thesis, science would soon come to an end. Without trustworthiness the finest laboratories would be relatively worthless. Science is a rare flower which grows only in certain well-prepared soil.

The most serious error in the calculation of those who argue from the principle of material causality to the denial of responsibility is the error of applying in the area of human actions a conception which is wholly appropriate on the nonhuman level, but is not, for that reason, necessarily appropriate on the human level. To apply to the moral decision of a man the same principles which are applied when we speak of the movement of a cloud or the salivation of a dog is to beg the crucial and difficult question of the uniqueness of man. If man has unique functions, as most serious thinkers have supposed, then there is no reason to suppose that the same conclusions follow in his case which follow when we deal with *things*.

We are close to the center of a constructive philosophy when we face seriously the evidence that human life is really unique in the world. Wonderful as is the physical object which the scientist observes, far more wonderful is the mind of the scientist *who is the observer*. Man is different from all other known creatures, not primarily in his body, which is similar to many others, and not absolutely in his intellectual processes, which some others share in degree, but in his capacity as a moral agent. Various higher animals use intelligence to secure ends which are dictated by appetite, but man has the unique capacity to choose between ends. Man is the creature who can say no to his appetites and often does so on the basis of moral considerations. The higher animals sometimes show genuine intelligence by the way they ask and answer the question, "How can I get it?" But man shows something beyond mere intelligence by his capacity to ask and answer the vastly different question, "Ought I to get it?" This is a difference so crucial that it must be termed a difference in kind rather than merely a difference in degree. The importance of this whole approach is recognized by the development of what is called philosophical anthropology, and especially by a succession of thinkers who realize that, unless the fact of man's essential differentiation is established, there is no effective answer to those who would deny moral responsibility in terms of a deterministic philosophy.[2]

There is a live alternative to the philosophy of moral escapism and, fortunately, this alternative has constituted the major thinking in the Western world. This philosophy rests squarely on the acceptance of responsibility which is an inescapable conclusion, providing we take choice seriously. The centrality and reality of responsibility are points on which the two major strands of our moral heritage, that which came from Greece and that which came from Palestine, are in agreement. The agreement is a rejection of fatalism in all its forms, in the conviction that all fatalism is inconsistent with the human experience of freedom, which no man really doubts in his own life, no matter how volubly he argues about it in others or the situation in general. The experience of freedom is the experience of the alteration of events, in part at least, by the effort to consider what is really right. It is difficult to see how any ethical life is possible in any other way. The great thinker who wrote the world's first manual on the science of ethics put the matter bluntly by saying, "It is truly absurd for a man to attribute his actions to external things."[3]

What will change the world for the better, if it is changed, is the action of men who accept, without complaint and without excuse, their own measure of responsibility for the state of the world and who believe that, by taking thought, a difference

[2] The problem of the uniqueness of man in nature is one which has interested me for many years and the one in which, under the direction of Prof. A. O. Lovejoy, I wrote my doctor's dissertation at Johns Hopkins University.

[3] *Nicomachean Ethics.* III, 1110b.

can be made. Only thus can we rise to the level of free men renouncing the easy doctrine that our acts are necessitated by external conditions. If we are free to act, we are responsible for our acts, but if we are not free, then all thought on this or any other subject is futile anyway. We are convinced that it is not futile.

If we accept the experience of freedom, in the sense of self-determination, as part of the truth about the world we are bound to be disturbed in mind. We cannot, then, blame all of our acts upon our childhood conditioning or upon the unavoidable influences of the external environment. Consequently we shall restore the uneasy conscience, which spurns the convenient way of escape from responsibility. It is one of the marks of a good man, as indeed it is a mark of a fully *mature* man, that he should be willing to stand up and say, "Yes. I did it. I am ashamed, but it was I who made the decision. I hope I may do better next time." If this tough-minded temper were to become general in our society we should be in a far more fortunate position than the one which we now hold.

There is nothing new about the idea that men differ on the question of what the good life involves and that whole societies have differed sharply on this point. What is new is the way in which the popular conclusion is drawn from these facts to the effect that one moral view is, therefore, as good as another. But there is no semblance of logical necessity for this conclusion. Of course men have differed about their duty, as they have differed about almost everything else, but this may merely show how easy it is to be *wrong*. Naturally it is easier to miss the target than to hit it! We can make mistakes about what we ought to do as we can make mistakes about any other matter.

The path of courage is not to give up the quest as impossible, but rather to use all the evidence we can collect and all the honest reasoning we can employ, to see what the evidence implies. When we differ we should be driven to deeper thought, because that is the only way in which the problem can be solved.

It is never easy to know what we ought to do, but there is no more helpful beginning than an honest effort to know *who* we are. Each individual is really an individual largely because of his unique set of relations, but every relation is also a *claim.* If I am a parent, then my relationship to my child constitutes a claim and one which I am never free to renounce. The same is true if I am a partner in marriage, a citizen, a borrower, a student, a teacher, a friend. I never know what I truly am until I know all of the relations which bind me to my fellows and my world.

When I really begin to understand who I am, I am well on the way to understanding what my duty, in any concrete situation, may be. Nothing is ever known completely in our necessarily finite experience, but we have sufficient light on our path to start, for to know in part is to know something. At least it is clear that I can never escape my responsibilities by the simple expedient of denying them, for they objectively *are.* If I am a debtor I do not have the same kind of financial freedom in investment which a man out of debt may have. If I am a creditor, I must fulfill a creditor's obligations and be willing to receive payment in the only way in which payment can be made. If I am a citizen, having willingly received many benefits and security, I cannot, with moral integrity, act suddenly as though this were not true.

When Socrates, having been condemned to die, was urged by his friend Crito to try to escape, the wise and good Athenian based his rejection of the suggestion on the effort to understand what his real relationship to the laws was. Socrates asked Crito to imagine that, as he was about to play truant, the laws should come to him and say: "Tell us, Socrates, what are you about? Are you not going by an act of yours to overturn us—the laws, and the whole state, as far as in you lies? Do you imagine that a state can subsist and not be overthrown, in which the decisions of law have no power, but are set aside and trampled upon by individuals?" The decisive conviction, so far as Socrates was concerned, arose from the realization that willingness to remain in Athens so long and to profit so much by its law and order, put him in a position in which he was no longer free to renounce his connection at will. His remaining there constituted an *implied contract* and a good man keeps his promises. This classic decision has become part of the moral heritage of Western man.

The integrity which we seek and which is at the apex of the moral life, comes by a delicate combination of individuality and solidarity, such as Socrates demonstrated. Far from living to ourselves alone, our very individuality arises from our unique responsibility to other men and to external causes. The man of integrity is the man of inner resources who can weather outer storms, but the inner resource is based upon connectedness with the totality of the external world. My station in life is not determined by me, but by my objective set of relations, yet when I really honor these relations, my individual duty is reasonably clear. It was a philosopher of the last generation, F. H. Bradley, who invented the term "My Station and its Duties"[4] and who showed persuasively that the clue to most of life's problems was found in this phrase, but the late William Temple stated the point in language which all can understand:

Membership of family and nation is not an accidental appendage of my individuality, but a constitutive element in it. It is always vain to say "If I had been a son of Napoleon Bonaparte" or any such thing. I *am* the son of my own father, and if he had had no son, but Napoleon had had an additional one, that means that someone else would have been born instead of me. Membership, such as carries with it a share in a common weal and woe, is an essential element in our nature.[5]

Important as is the acceptance of responsibility for ourselves, it cannot end there. Individual peace is not enough and individual integrity is not possible unless it includes concern for our neighbors far and near. It is essential to the good life, which we are trying to describe, that we are our brothers' keepers. It is not that we must interfere, in a meddling way, with what is the business of other people, but rather that we recognize the way in which our lives are inextricably intermingled.

Personality is glorified and comes into its own, not by independence, but rather by such a glad acceptance of claims that the emphasis is on the responsibilities of the self rather than the deserts of the self. Robert Louis Stevenson, who took pride in being a "lay moralist," expressed this position in manly words when he wrote to his publisher:

The world must return someday to the word "duty" and be done with the word "reward." There are no rewards, and

[4] F. H. Bradley, *Ethical Studies*, Essay V.
[5] William Temple, *Nature Man and God* (London: Macmillan, 1934), pp. 186, 187.

plenty duties. And the sooner a man sees that and acts upon it, like a gentleman or a fine old barbarian, the better for himself.

There is a great danger in our contemporary emphasis on the division of labor which so easily becomes a division of responsibility. The tendency is for the technician to say, "The use to which this instrument is put is no concern of mine; my only responsibility is to *make* it." In the same way the private citizen may go on peacefully about his affairs, leaving government to the experts. That this is the road which leads to moral decay is shown by much evidence, some of the most striking evidence being provided by preHitler Germany.

Freedom from guilt has been considered, in our time, on too much of an individualistic basis. The sense of guilt, which has been damaging to some, and which the doctrines we have been examining have sought to eliminate, has usually referred merely to conventional personal infractions of the moral law. We need to go much further and develop a beneficent sense of guilt for our social failures as a people. This is especially appropriate in regard to our failure to provide equality of opportunity and the material basis of a decent life for our fellow men, wherever they are. The terrible waste of money and time and resources, which we have come to assume as standard in modern government, is immoral not merely because of the self-indulgence of the officials concerned, but far more because of the needs of men and women who could have been aided by these same resources and by this same time and money. The human race is not so rich that it can afford the luxury of waste.

If we take seriously the philosophy of the West, which is the philosophy of responsibility, we must recognize the burden which comes in necessary association with privilege. The greater the power at our disposal the greater is our responsibility to use it wisely and well for the general good. To whom much is given, of him much is required. We are the people of earth who have the great opportunity of a rich cumulative inheritance of ideas, plus the gains in manner of living which modern science and technology make possible. Accordingly there are available to us tremendous resources, so that we can perform, in some areas, what would seem like miracles to the majority of the earth's inhabitants. It is essential to our Western moral ideal that these advantages must never be used for ourselves alone and that we recognize that *they are given to us in trust. What men ought to give is determined by their abilities; what men ought to receive is determined by their needs.* Great advantages, far from giving us easy minds, should give us very *uneasy* minds. If the philosophy of responsibility is true our burden is heavy; if it is not true, there isn't anything that we can do anyway.

IV

THE ACHIEVEMENT OF FREEDOM

Man is most free in the discovery that he is not free.
—REINHOLD NIEBUHR

There is no word in the vocabulary of Western man that is used today with greater honor than the word "freedom." It is our proud claim that *our* half of the world is the free world, by which we mean that we have freedom of speech, of religion, of assembly and of criticism. Though freedom is something which all peoples of the world claim to prize, it seems to belong to us in a peculiar sense and with a certain justification. Those on the other side of the World Civil War claim to uphold democracy, by which is meant economic rather than political democracy, but they do not even make any pretense of complete freedom of thought and expression. Indeed, they reject such freedom as something decadent. We, on the other hand, have tended to exalt a particular kind of freedom so much that we make it the supreme or sometimes the only value.

We have inherited, in the modern Western world, as a legacy from the French Revolution, the threefold slogan—Liberty, Equality and Fraternity—and, having so often heard these words in conjunction, we assume that they are naturally part of a single ideal, but in fact they have no necessary connection. Two of them, equality and liberty, far from being necessarily joined, are often incompatible with each other. There are many situations, particularly economic ones, in which it is easy to secure equality, providing we give up freedom. By forming a labor union we can guarantee equal wages, but usually we pay for this the stiff human price of restricting the freedom of some, and particularly of the gifted and energetic, to achieve results above the level of mediocrity. On the other hand, it is relatively easy to give freedom, in the sense of unrestricted opportunity to advance economically, providing we are not greatly concerned about equality. If we permit unrestrained freedom of enterprise we soon have a situation in which the contrasts between rich and poor are enormous, with many left insecure. The combination of full equality and full liberty is apparently an impossible combination.

All words that are widely used tend to be ambiguous, but the word "freedom" suffers in this way to an unusual degree. The word has so many metaphysical, moral and economic meanings that many people can claim to be in favor of freedom and actually be widely separated in their fundamental thinking. Since there is nothing sacred about definitions, anyone is permitted to use the word as he likes, providing he is consistent in doing so, but clarification may come by deeper thought on the primary issues which any use of the word raises.

While those who accept the Russian philosophy reject most Western conceptions of freedom, they claim to have some of their own. When their armies go into new territory they claim to go as liberators, the presumption being that they set people free from capitalist domination. They deny, however, the right of free speech and freedom of ownership, because the former, they think, undermines the orderliness of the regime, while the latter, if allowed, would destroy the communist economy. They refuse to tolerate a vigorous Church for the same reason that they refuse to tolerate any other serious internal criticism. Only one philosophy can be taught because, they hold, only one is true, and all others are in error. They think it is absurd to give freedom to error to propagate itself.

The Russian system not only denies the freedoms we prize as a matter of practical strategy, but, what is far more important, denies the reality of metaphysical freedom as well. This can be stated confidently, inasmuch as the Russians and their satellites have an agreed and published dogma. The dogma is that freedom of choice is a delusion. All events, including thoughts, are determined, and they are determined by a complex material situation. It is claimed that this conclusion is simply the scientific one and that all contrasting views are unscientific. At first it looks as though this makes the scientific social experimenter free to mold events according to an ideal and thus be liberated from chance or from an arbitrary divine will, but, as we have pointed out in the preceding chapter, it leaves no freedom at all, not even to the one conducting the experiment. If the determinist philosophy is true, the experimenter himself was wholly determined, in that prior physical conditions *caused him* to perform the precise experiment he mistakenly supposed he had personally decided to make.

In this terrifying conception of life there is no escape from fatalism, and fatalism, in the natural course of events, produces tyranny. Men may still *feel* free, in some of their planning, but, if they are consistent, they are forced to admit that even their apparent freedom of thought is an illusion, because it is brute matter that is solely responsible for their ideals and their apparent decisions. Thus each man and each society lives and must live in the stifling world of necessity. There is no escape from social conditioning which, once it is perfectly established, will make even government unnecessary, in that men can be so conditioned that they will no longer seek to revolt. Though the language of the West is still employed in this system, what is actually involved is a reversal to the ancient fatalism which antedated the use of the free spirit in Greece. In a world in which decision, as a result of free thought, undetermined by any force outside the character of the person, has no meaning, it is not surprising that such secondary forms of freedom as freedom of speech and freedom of assembly are denied, because, in the long run, the philosophical position determines the practical positions. Thus tyranny follows fatalism by inner necessity.

On our side of the Civil War the tendency is for the people to be as extreme in maintaining freedom, both practical and metaphysical, as the people on the other side are extreme in the renunciation of it. There are, of course, a few, particularly those who work in the social sciences, who deny any freedom of the will, but they have scarcely touched the popular mentality. The majority believe that they actually make their own decisions and they propose to criticize the government or anyone else in authority and to grumble as much as they please. We have now, for many months, had a running debate on foreign policy, in which thousands have taken part, and, though some might look upon this as weakness, most of us are convinced that it is really our glory. The most important fact about the public debate is that it is still possible. There is no external authority to decide it for us.

We have a profound faith, already justified by much experience, that the good life is more likely to come when we keep a stubborn tension between the claims of individual dignity and the claims of organization. Thus we have laws, but some of the laws are enacted to provide for the consciences of those who cannot accept the conclusions or practices of the majority. We understand a great deal about the moral ideal of the Western world when we note that Britain, in the midst of her bitterest struggle in the second World War, when invasion was expected daily, gave full exemption from military duty to many men who refused to participate in war on grounds of religious conscience. Any system which can include freedom at this level has the seeds of greatness in it and is worth preserving.

The chief reason why the maintenance of the freedom to criticize is so important is that man by nature is highly fallible, and this applies to all men, including those who are in authority. The freedom essential to democracy rests, not on the conviction that men are always trustworthy, but rather on the realistic observation that often they are *not* trustworthy. The reason why a system of checks and balances is needed in any society, and why a society without these will eventually fall into decay, is that all men are potentially corrupt and that *this includes the leaders*. Men who were perfect, and who could reach the truth infallibly, would not need to have internal criticism in the system they might guide, but we do not know of the existence of any such men. Freedom is therefore not an adornment, but is required for the achievement of the good life because all men are in the finite predicament. The freedom of democracy is the best way of life, not because all men are virtuous and reasonable, for they are not, but because all men are greedy for power. The freedom of thought and expression, which leads to freedom of criticism, provides a curb on the wanton exercise of power, either in a government or in an individual man. The fatal flaw in all totalitarianism arises from its failure to be thorough in its view of man. It not only fails to reckon with the potential nobility of human nature in modest circumstances, but, even more, it fails to make a thorough application of its own doctrine of human corruptibility. It sees that the masses are corrupt, but it refuses to face the corruptibility of the tyrant himself, who, like all others, shares in the human situation. Democracy is more thoroughgoing, in that it recognizes the universality of human weakness, and therefore gives the common man a check upon the uncommon man. How well the Founding Fathers knew this is shown by the words of George Washington who, in his Farewell Address, based his entire argument for constitutional restraints upon the need of "a just estimate of that love of power, and proneness to abuse it, which predominates in the human heart." Democracy is necessitated by the fact that all men are sinners; it is made possible by the fact that we know it.

Since there are usually several ways of missing the mark, it is wholly possible that Western man has ways of missing the fullest understanding of freedom in one direction, while Eastern man misses it in another. *Our* danger is not the Marxist denial of freedom in favor of a totalitarian scheme, but rather the espousal of a kind of freedom which is purely negative and which may eventually become self-destructive. Millions, when they assert their faith in freedom, mean to say that they believe it is the natural right of every man to do exactly as he pleases under all circumstances. The popular position in the West is the opinion that freedom, in the sense of the elimination of all inhibitions on personal action, is a natural right and ought not to be denied to anyone. On all sides is the cry, "Let me alone. Let me do as I please. Let me live my own life as I like."

Such a conception of freedom has numerous exponents in nearly all of our student communities, particularly since the war, and almost every academic administration has had to face attacks from this quarter. Student government has been rendered particularly difficult, and difficult on what is really an ideological basis. Several universities have found that this ideology has made anything in the nature of an honor system absolutely untenable. It is obviously untenable if one of the freedoms espoused is the freedom to cheat. The scandals of college athletics, especially in the bribery of star players, are not isolated events, but are logical extensions of the popular view of what freedom means. These weak young men are now supposedly in disgrace because they took large sums of money, to enable the gambling barons to make enormous bets with complete assurance concerning the outcome of the games, but we ought to face the fact that these young men were merely putting into practice a doctrine which so many others tacitly espouse. Certainly there would not be this kind of bribery apart from the gambling, and there would be no gambling barons apart from the thousands in ordinary life who believe that freedom includes the freedom to bet. The young men were merely demonstrating their freedom to take bribes! Perhaps the most disturbing part of the whole degrading episode was the continued high standing of these young men in the eyes of their fellow students.

The popular idea which is widely espoused, even though we

are a bit shocked when it is acted upon with consistency, is that freedom comes by the simple process of rejecting everything, whether of law, of custom, or of moral standard, that seems to hinder a person in securing the pleasure of the moment or fulfilling his immediate desires. The notion is that freedom is a right, with no necessary relations to duties; it stands alone as the supreme good and, as such, is the heritage of every man and woman. Above all, such freedom is believed to be *cheap*; there is little thought that it may be something which must be earned.

Since it is part of this idea that a sense of duty is somehow stultifying, we propose to escape it by the simple road of denying its claims. The characteristic men and women of this generation in the West, revolting understandably against the sternness of an older code, have been eager to live their own lives, to do as they please, to throw off all inhibitions, and suddenly they have their reward! They get what they seek, but it is not so attractive in possession as it is in prospect. They think they are emancipated when they are merely unbuttoned. They have the spurious freedom of one who does not know where he is going or to what he belongs. And, insofar as this is a candid picture of our time, we are a lost generation. We are free in the sense that a ship is free when it has lost both compass and rudder.

From this spurious freedom come all kinds of human ills. The freedom to flounder accentuates the bondage to self which in many instances is all that is left. Then we become concerned with our own advancement, our own health, and the satisfaction of our own appetites. Thousands in this sad situation, feeling fundamentally insecure, rush from one fashionable resort to another, when they can afford to do so, hoping thereby to regain a vanished youth or to find some new interest. Marriages break up because one or both of the partners has "the desire to be happy," the determination to live their own lives as they like or the comforting conviction that the difficulty lies in the failure of the other partner. But the tragedy is that, in general, the new marriage has some of the same difficulties of the old one.

We may, indeed, take marriage as a test case in the effort to understand the contemporary human situation, because it is nearly universal and because the evidence of failure is so widespread and so difficult to hide. The conditions which make possible a stable and mutually satisfying marriage are not merely physical ones. It will be generally conceded that mutual sexual satisfaction is normally necessary for a successful and enduring marriage, but we delude ourselves terribly if we suppose that this satisfaction is merely a matter of physical responsiveness or attractiveness. It is far more a willingness to transcend self-centeredness in concern for the welfare of one's partner, but that is a *moral* consideration and a limitation on the individual. Moreover, successful marriage requires far more than what are popularly known as psychological factors.

It is true that some temperaments are more easily harmonized than others, but temperamental affinity will not carry men and women very far; it will not even carry them successfully through the honeymoon. Old-fashioned as it may sound, we must face the fact that no enduringly successful marriage is possible without the introduction of moral control on both sides. Marriage between moral adolescents, each bent on complete self-expression, will *always* fail, and it will fail miserably. It will fail because life together is as difficult as it is glorious and therefore requires daily effort to restrain selfish desires out of consideration for the beloved.

Many have sought, in our day, to popularize the idea that moral considerations are outdated and that life is very much more pleasant without these hindrances to self-expression, but when we practice this comforting doctrine, either in the home or in the state, we run into disaster. The acceptance of freedom as freedom from all restraint would be as damaging to democracy as to the home. Freedom, so interpreted, would give a man the right to do as he pleased with his private property, even if that property were human beings. Indeed, some of Lincoln's opponents in the slavery controversy, immediately prior to the Civil War, based their entire argument on this conception of freedom, which, as they logically inferred, was incompatible with any kind of limitation on the *owners*. In his famous debate with Judge Douglas, Lincoln expressed this position as follows: "It is, as a principle, no other than that if one man chooses to make a slave of another man, neither that other man nor anybody else has a right to object."[1]

The notion that slavery could ever be defended on the basis of a belief in freedom seems absurd to us now, but the very fact that men could ever argue in this way is a vivid demonstration of the inherent contradiction which freedom understood as freedom from all restraint contains. It is not a matter of what we like, but of what is possible for man. And the truth is that it is not possible to carry on a satisfactory life at any human level without self-restraint, without consideration for what is right and wrong, and without consideration for the rights and liberties of others.

[1] *Letters and Speeches of Abraham Lincoln*, Everyman Edition, p. 136.

We cannot make even a start in the direction of a good life for all unless we understand that this oversimple notion of freedom, now so popular in the life of the West, is nonsense. The chief reason why it is nonsense is found in the realistic observation that no man is an isolated individual, and, since different members of the same society have conflicting desires, there is no real possibility even of the bare continuation of life, let alone anything in the nature of a good life, unless we do restrain ourselves for the sake of our fellows and our relations to them. Every person has many desires which, if they were immediately satisfied, would be disastrous in results. We may, for example, desire the other man's possessions. Are we therefore to throw off all restraints and follow the path of freedom in taking possession? Few, who espouse the doctrine of freedom mentioned above, actually go this far, but logically, there is no good reason why they should not do so.

The thousands who travel each year to Reno and get easy divorces go because they are restive under the restraints of married life and want to be free. At least that is what they say of themselves. But what is good for a few, ought, in consistency, to be good for all. Why should not any man, with a wife and children, do the same, when he finds home life restrictive in any degree? After all, the burdens of rearing and supporting a family are great and the personal sacrifices are many. They keep a man in pretty tight harness, sending him daily to the office or factory. He could become "free" by walking out someday and not returning. Or, made restive by the restraints of monogamy, he might develop a strong attachment to his secretary or some other woman acquaintance and leave his home for the sake of this new attachment. Is there anything in the superficial doctrine of freedom which, of itself, would avoid this result? Of course such an action would bring hardship and shame upon his children, but that is a consideration of a totally different kind. If the rule of freedom is in itself an adequate rule, there is nothing to stop such action, since a man in that position would be "living his own life" and "expressing his individuality." Multiply this illustration by millions and the result is chaos and anarchy which destroy both the peace and happiness of all concerned.

The most obvious difficulty about freedom, as popularly taught in the West, is the fact that many different freedoms are mutually incompatible. My freedom to *take* the other man's goods or the other man's job or the other man's wife is incompatible with his freedom to *keep* them; the freedom of a student to cheat in an examination is incompatible with the freedom of the others in the class to have a fair system of grading; the freedom of the man who wishes to play his musical instrument all night is incompatible with the freedom of his neighbors to sleep. Such illustrations could be multiplied endlessly, because we live in the kind of world in which there is no possibility of order without concern for the rights of others, which means that there must always be restraints, which means that simple freedom, far from being a natural right, is a manifest absurdity.

Fantastic as such an idea of freedom may become when subjected to analysis, it nevertheless has a great hold on the modern mind and has already done incalculable harm. This is most clear in our economic system where the constant emphasis is on rights rather than on duties and responsibilities. We thus develop an entire cast of mind in which workers of all levels tend to have an eye on the clock, with the primary attention to what they are to get and little or no attention to what they can give. In the long run it is an intangible force of this character that determines the destiny of a people or the fortunes of a civilization, just as truly as it is determined by physical factors such as natural resources and geography. The doctrine becomes a blight upon our total life and, if we are realistic, we shall do all we can to destroy it because we know that the philosophy of a people is bound to affect its actions.

What we require, not merely for the sake of our moral life, but for the sake of all other phases of our existence, is a deeper and more realistic understanding of how freedom is possible. As we think about it, we soon begin to appreciate the important truth that *freedom is something that must be earned*. Unearned freedom is always false and delusive freedom. Consider, for example, the consumption of alcoholic drinks, which play such an increasing part in the modern world that, in America at least, we spend far more money annually on alcohol as a beverage than we spend on all education from the kindergarten to professional school. It may be generally conceded that the ideal is freedom to use or not to use alcoholic drinks and that the mark of the true drunkard is that his action is compulsive. When the alcoholic reaches for the glass he is not demonstrating his self-determination, but his lack of it, because the mark of the genuine alcoholic is that *he cannot resist*. Something other than his own will is driving him. But the person who *can* resist, and is therefore free, is the person who has schooled himself and lives an ordered life. This disciplined freedom is not merely appropriated, but must be achieved, often by much effort. The man who does not say "no" to his appetites, far from being free in the practical sense of maintaining in his life the possibility of rational choice, is really a person held in terrible bondage.

There is a curious meeting of extremes, in that the empty freedom of the West and the fatalism of the East both make it unnecessary for a man to concern himself with an objective moral order. The person who pays no attention to an objective moral order appears to have, superficially, a freedom of action that is denied the person who is bound by such an order. Thus the notorious Russian statesman, Jacob Malik, whose presidency of the Security Council of the United Nations in August, 1950, will long be remembered, had a species of freedom denied his fellow members on the Council. The others, presumably, in referring to the bitter struggle in Korea, felt required to pay some attention to verifiable facts about the original aggression, but Mr. Malik appeared to be emancipated from anything so restrictive. He, it seemed, could be really single-minded, since apparently the only consideration he had to keep in mind was the effect of propaganda, especially on the Chinese. The others were seriously restricted, in referring to the participation of Chinese troops, by the facts of the case, but Mr. Vishinsky, like his colleague, had no need to bother with that. Indeed, there is no important reason why such speeches as these diplomats made could not have been composed before the event. It is clear that, if such practices were generally espoused, the world would become a madhouse. With the complete substitution of strategic advantage or propaganda effect, for objective truth, all trustworthiness would go out of the world and it is difficult to see how the business of civilization could go forward at all.

The paradox is that the two theories of freedom, currently

popular on the two sides of the World Civil War, different as they appear superficially, actually produce startlingly similar results. It is easy to see that Stalinism leads to tyranny, but we have been slow to see that our debased vision leads in the same direction. The man who refuses to limit his action by moral considerations is acting exactly as a tyrant seeks to act, for the essence of a tyrant's life, as Plato saw long ago, is the desire to "do as you like."[2]

The chief danger of the concept of freedom which is now so fashionable is that it can so easily become a preparation for the entire denial of personal freedom which we call totalitarianism, because men may actually seek *Escape from Freedom*. Sensing the confusion which mere negative freedom produces, men in despair become easy marks for a totalitarian propaganda; they give their lives away to some external or powerful authority, which does their thinking and makes their decisions for them. Then, with a reassuring feeling of solidarity in a community, not dissimilar to that of the hive, they march happily and thoughtlessly on to doom. *The errors of the thesis lead directly to the errors of the antithesis.* We must never forget that many of those who became Hitler's staunchest upholders were those very "Wandering Birds," wearing short trousers and playing guitars, who finally became so tired of their meaningless freedom that they actually welcomed the mental slavery of Hitlerism.

We have seen that freedom in the negative sense is an insupportable idea because it leads to all sorts of confusion and contradictions. We must look for a justifiable conception, therefore, in the realm of *positive* freedom. This is freedom to

[2] *The Laws*, II, p. 661.

act in *the light of a valid ideal*, and therefore to resist the whims and fancies of the passing moment, which, if all were followed, would destroy any life or lead to the madhouse. Part of our unexploited cultural wealth lies in the fact that our great tradition in the West has never upheld the freedom of which we speak so easily and so much, but has been of a radically different order. Schiller was speaking for the great tradition when he said, "*Freiheit bedeutet nicht, dass jeder tun kann was er will, sondern dass er werden kann, was er soll*—Freedom does not mean that everyone can do as he likes, but that he can become what he should." The ancient doctrine is that there is something as far beyond empty freedom as it is beyond authoritarianism, and this is the freedom which comes by loyal recognition of the objective moral order which is not altered by our passing whims.

The freedom which comes from such recognition is magnificently illustrated in the life of marital fidelity, which is actually more *liberating* than is the life of the philanderer, because the loyal man is relieved of the constant necessity of deciding whether he will seek to court every attractive woman he sees. *Having made one great decision, and being resolutely loyal to it, he is free from the strain of constant new choices.* If we were to make new choices every moment on every subject, from honesty to industry, we should soon be insane. The ability to choose is part of man's glory, but that glory is dimmed unless there are some fundamental choices which are *regulative* in the sense that they determine in advance a host of minor decisions and make their conscious operation unnecessary.

The kind of freedom which is not finally self-contradictory, and therefore self-destructive, is that in which men and women are encouraged, in spite of their finite limitations, to make it their main business to undertake an enlightened effort to know what is really right and to do it. The truly free man is the one in whom the sensitive conscience is regulative of total conduct. Man is made of many parts and freedom comes when these parts have the proper relation to one another, each fulfilling its own function. Man's life is dignified when he becomes loyal to what he has reason to believe is an objective principle, which can dominate the passing moment, often keeping a person at some difficult labor, not because he likes the drudgery and not because he would not welcome release, but because he is loyal to something about which he cares more than he cares for his own bodily ease or comfort.

The most important secret of freedom in this higher sense of positive freedom, which is "freedom to" rather than "freedom from," is the acceptance of discipline. Discipline is the price of freedom and the only road by which it may be anywhere achieved. This truth is very hard for modern man to understand and accept. Since we have supposedly outgrown Puritanism and all its works, are we really advised, the critic asks, to turn the clock back to that chapter of Western life? The answer is that we can never turn any clock back, so far as human development is concerned, but we realize that not all knowledge was born with us and that our ancestors have much to teach us. Part of our intellectual cheapness is shown by the fact that, popularly, we have been grossly unfair in our attack upon Puritanism, the method of attack being to make a caricature and then find it easy to destroy. Insofar as the Puritan ideal is that of the controlled and ordered life, as against wanton self-indulgence, and this was the inspiring principle of thousands in the seventeenth century, when our experiment was young, this ideal is a permanent element in any good life that men or women are likely to enjoy on this planet.

Though our tendency is to resist the claims of discipline in moral experience, they are widely accepted in other areas, notably in science, in athletics and in art. Everyone knows that no person can achieve excellence in any art without a long and laborious discipline. Most writers must discipline their style for years before what they write is worth printing. The young musician must burden himself and his family with the seemingly endless hours of practice, but, if he succeeds in really disciplining his fingers, his hearing and his vocal chords, he is set free in a way in which no undisciplined person is ever free. He is truly liberated. The undisciplined person may sit at a piano, but he is not free to strike the notes he would like to strike; he is not free because he has not paid the necessary price of this particular freedom. Here is a convincing illustration of the principle that freedom is something to be achieved rather than something appropriated with ease as a natural inheritance.

All who have any touch with scientific enterprises know what a large part discipline plays in this realm. Indeed science, as the practicing scientist knows it, is not a set of beliefs or a compendium of fixed conclusions, but a *method*. It is a disciplined way of thinking, acting and verifying, which becomes so central to the scientist's whole life that he habitually looks at all situations with an eye to *evidence*. It is only by long discipline of thought and hand that he is able to know when genuine verification occurs. The most dependable man in a scientific dispute is the man who has been over this rough road, learning to judge what the evidence really is, uninfluenced by what would be desirable or what any preconceived opinion might dictate.

We cannot resist the conclusion that moral development comes in the same way. In the end we are forced to depend upon ethical judgments, and in these men differ, but we cannot leave the matter there any more than we are satisfied to rest when we are faced with conflicting scientific judgments. The most trustworthy judgment is always the judgment of those who have submitted themselves, not only to discipline, but to the *appropriate* and the *relevant* discipline. Until this is understood and accepted the desire for freedom, far from being a boon to mankind, is always a source of confusion and ultimately of despair.

Our task is to try to establish in the popular mind, before it is too late, a philosophy of discipline that is as far from bondage to self as it is from totalitarian bondage. The middle ground, which is our security against the excesses of both the right and the left, is the ground of *self*-discipline. We must teach again the nobility of that kind of life in which men and women so control themselves for the sake of an ideal or for the welfare of all, that they glory in the very hardness of their lives. We must make prevail a conception of life in which men are proud of a Stoic sternness and glad for a life marked by inner restraints. We must encourage a pattern according to which men are ashamed of soft and self-centered living and are not ashamed of lives which show the marks of purposive control.

There is good reason to believe that our world is one in which right and wrong are not human inventions or the mere projections, on a cosmic screen, of our subjective wishes. There is the same reason to believe in moral law that there is to believe in natural law, though the one may be harder to discern than the other. What we require is far more disciplined effort to determine what this moral law is and a wave of sentiment according to which moral considerations seem important. Otherwise we are not likely to have the freedom which we suppose we prize, but which we so inadequately understand. What the chief principles of the moral order really are we do not know in any complete sense, but we can be relatively certain of a few points and to one of these we give our attention in the following chapter.

V

RESPECT FOR PERSONS

The principle of morality is that we should behave as Persons who are members of a Society of Persons—a Society into which Personality is itself a valid claim of entrance.

—WILLIAM TEMPLE

The most important fact which faces any person who is struggling with the problem of living is the fact that there are other persons in the world. If, as a popular novel suggests, there were a plague so widespread that one man were to find himself alone, most of the ethical wisdom of mankind would be wholly irrelevant, because this wisdom is chiefly concerned with right relations with our neighbors, near and far. It is these other persons who give us our greatest joy, as they give us our greatest pain. They provide our chief opportunity for achievement and they constitute our chief problem. A world devoid of other persons would not involve any major difficulties, but neither would it involve the possibility of a really meaningful existence. The right relations to others is not the whole of ethics, but it is the most of it. There are some duties which a man owes to himself, but they are relatively simple ones, whereas nearly all the duties and responsibilities which we owe to others are amazingly complex. The verbs which, according to the elementary Latin rule take the dative, words meaning to *believe, favor, help, please, trust;* also to *command, obey, par-*

don, persuade, resist, serve and *spare*, indicate something of the level on which most lives are lived. All of these common verbs represent relations which are transitive and all require objects which are persons. We spend part of our time working with things, making things and repairing things, but normally we work in groups and, even in manufacturing enterprises, the hardest problems are personal ones. Difficult as it was for men to learn the secrets of physics, sufficiently to be able to produce atomic fission, this task was by no means as difficult as that of finding trustworthy men to share the secrets of production. We succeeded magnificently in the physical problem, but we failed dismally in the human problem! This illustration, now so vividly in the consciousness of our day, is a most revealing one in that it demonstrates the inescapability of the human problem. There is no possibility of science without scientists, but the chief problems of scientists are their problems as *men*, rather than their problems as scientists. The major reason why we are able to handle the resources of physical nature so much better than we handle the resources of moral nature is not that one group of intellectual workers in the world is so much more able than another, but rather that one set of problems is so much more simple than the other.

What we seek, as we face the task of living with other people, is some guiding principle which may help to bring order out of our daily confusion. This has been sought for centuries by some of the best minds which our race has known and these have left us a garnered wisdom. Frequently we have been very slow, in our total culture, to apply with any adequacy the principles already accepted, but the application does come at last. As was mentioned in an earlier chapter, it took eighteen hundred years for men to see that the principle of the infinite value of every human soul made human slavery untenable, but at last the application came. It is wholly possible that there are other applications, quite as inevitable, but that we have not yet become conscious of them. The moral as well as the physical universe is wider than our views of it.

The reasonable way to approach the question of *ought* is by a deeper understanding of *is*. "To other animals, ignorance of themselves is natural," says Boethius, "in men it is a fault." If we know what man is, we are well on the way to the knowledge of how he should be treated. We say that a man is a *person*, by which we mean that he is a creature who is self-conscious, that he can say "no" to his appetites out of a sense of duty, that he has a sense of the distinction between right and wrong, that he appreciates values. Many other creatures have minds and some of the higher ones, notably the primates, are capable of reason, but man can do what a mere reasoning creature cannot do. The mere reasoning creature may employ thought to achieve ends which the appetites seek, but man is really a person in the sense that he asks whether he *ought* to seek and to achieve these ends. As was pointed out in Chapter III, the two questions, "How can I get it?" and "Ought I to get it?" are questions so different that they differ in kind. They do not belong to the same universe of discourse. The capacity to ask meaningfully the second question is always and everywhere the distinguishing mark of personality. Man began when this question was first asked.

It is clear that it is by means of the capacities just described, rather than by any physical characteristics, that man differs from all other inhabitants of earth. The physical differences are not really very great and certainly do not warrant, of themselves, the claim of absolute uniqueness on man's part. Other creatures have hands, others have large brains in comparison to bodily weight, others have a nearly erect posture. The essence of man, therefore, must lie in his qualities as a *person*. It may be part of the wisdom about life to take our unique characteristics seriously and stress them more than we do. Man, for example, is the only animal who laughs, and it is a good thing to accentuate this aspect of uniqueness. There is a time to laugh just as there is a time to refrain from laughter.

The development of personality is something that has come late on the earth, and at the climax of a long development. The earth was in existence long before there were men on it, and likewise the earth was inhabited long before men joined the other inhabitants. Man, when he appeared, appeared in an already going world. If we follow the available evidence we must conclude that, for a long period, the earth was merely a material unit with wind and weather and tides, but no life. Vegetable life appeared first and was followed much later by animal life, with its remarkable capacity for movement and finally for consciousness, in the sense of awareness of the environment. Personality, as already described, was quite as signal an advance over animal life as life itself had been over mere matter. The history of our planet, therefore, has been the history of a series of levels, in which each level surpasses its predecessor, yet each depends upon its predecessors and would be meaningless without them. The higher levels presuppose the lower ones, but the lower do not presuppose the higher. The most striking way in which the levels appear is as follows:

1. Unconsciousness
2. Consciousness
3. Self-consciousness

As we contemplate the significance of self-consciousness, we begin to have some hints of why it is that man can rise to such heights of self-sacrifice and sink to such depths of shame. Only a self-conscious creature could say "no" to his own appetites and be penitent for his own acts, but, conversely, only a self-conscious creature could be so driven by overweening pride and lust for power that he would bring misery to millions of his innocent fellow humans. Other creatures, like the peacock, have vanity, but man alone has pride. Vanity is the parading of what has been given, but pride involves satisfaction in what we have, ourselves, produced. This leads to great advances, but also to great human misery. We can never tell the truth about man as person in a single sentence, because paradox is intrinsic in his nature. If we tell only of the greatness of man we give a false impression, but if we tell only of the littleness of man we give an equally false impression. He is at once both noble and base and part of his nobility is the recognition, *by himself*, of his baseness. The sharp words of Blaise Pascal constitute the classic statement of this theme, especially in the following aphorism:

The greatness of man is great in that he knows himself to be miserable. A tree does not know itself to be miserable. It is then being miserable to know oneself to be miserable, but it is also being great to know that one is miserable.

It is this strange and endlessly interesting phenomenon, personality, which seems to have been the goal toward which the

only part of the universe with which we are intimately acquainted has, for millions of years, been pointing. We do not
know, of course, what has been occurring on other planets or
in other solar systems, nor do we know what the final outcome
of our planetary history may be. It is always possible that the
later stages of the earth's history may present some phenomenon as much advanced beyond personality as personality is
advanced beyond mere life, but that is a matter of fruitless
speculation. It is, however, a reasonable inference that any
future development of this kind, continuing the cumulative
pattern already established, will go *beyond* personality and not
against it. If the higher stages continue to employ and transcend
the lower, as life employs and transcends matter, we may reasonably infer that personality, far from being a meaningless incident, lies in the main line of advance. Growth will then be
through it and not *around* it nor *against* it.

For practical purposes the chief point to note is the absolute
difference between persons and things. Things may rightly be
used as implements, partly because they have no consciousness
and the element of pain is not involved. Moreover, in the sub-
personal levels individuality is never a primary factor. It is
doubtless true that no two snowflakes are identical and that no
two leaves on a tree are exactly alike, but their similarities are
so great that, for most practical purposes, the differences can
be neglected without consequent loss. Two pieces of anthracite
coal from the same mine may not be identical in chemical formation, but they are near enough for purposes of scientific analysis. Thus in a laboratory we use one sample and then discard
it, recognizing that the samples do not have intrinsic value.
Since their value is not intrinsic, it is instrumental, and the

recognition of this fact is what makes the experimental method possible. We cannot experiment with that which is infinitely precious, in the sense that each individual counts supremely, but we *can* experiment when individuality is an unimportant factor.

The dividing line between the areas in which experimentation is justifiable and the areas in which it is not justifiable is one of the most significant dividing lines in the world. Below that line the group characteristics of objects are more significant than are the individual characteristics, while above that line the individual characteristics are more significant than the group characteristics. There is, of course, some argument as to just where this line falls, but there is no denying that it falls somewhere. Even the person who opposes vivisection agrees to the wisdom of experimentation on plants and Dr. Albert Schweitzer, though reverence for life is the central plank of his philosophy, admits the rightness of vivisection under certain conditions or with certain safeguards.

Whatever we may think of experiments on animals, the combined conscience of mankind recognizes that it is wrong to treat men and women as mere guinea pigs. If a man voluntarily submits to an experiment, as in some new treatment of disease, we are bound to honor his heroism in a marked degree, but it is everywhere wrong to make men and women the involuntary subjects of experiments, because that is to debase their innate dignity; it is to use them as mere instruments when their essential nature is such that each requires separate and unique respect. It follows that we must never treat men as mere parts of a machine, because humanity is not mechanical. The significance of each man lies not so much in the fact that he is one more example of the human species, but rather that each is really unique, a locus of individual desires and hopes and aspirations, and that this very individuality is the essential feature of the situation. It is the nature of mechanics that the machine may have interchangeable parts, but there is nothing really correlative to this in the life of human beings.

What is infinitely precious is not the mere biological organism, tender as we ought to be with it, but rather the person as a conscious center of value and of valuing. There is no sounder or more often quoted philosophical insight than that of Socrates when he said that the unexamined life is not worth living. Every decent man is aware that there are many situations in which he would gladly sacrifice his own life for something he values more. What is prized is not mere survival, but survival of a particular *kind*, both for ourselves and for others.

If these principles just enunciated are true, we must always renounce the notion that some human beings are "expendable" as our flippant military phrase puts it. Some men are evil; some men are weak; but no men are expendable. It is everywhere wrong to treat men as though they were mechanical parts, coming into an assembly line, and one of the greatest evils of war is the fact that this treatment of men seems almost inevitable in the midst of the battle.

We speak much of democracy, sometimes suggesting that it is merely a political device, but it means almost nothing unless it is firmly grounded in some such view of man as we are trying in this chapter to present. It was part of the greatness of Abraham Lincoln that he recognized this deeper basis and referred to it constantly. His opponents ridiculed him because of his frequent references to the words of the Declaration of Independence, to the effect that all men are created equal. They pointed out, knowingly, that men are not equal in brains or in strength or in natural gifts and that Negroes are conspicuously inferior to white people in a number of respects. Lincoln countered by fully admitting such factual inequality, but held that the fundamental equality is that of the dignity which belongs to a human being, whatever his strength or talents. Of the black man, Lincoln said:

In the right to put into his mouth the bread that his own hands have earned, he is the equal of every other man, white or black. In pointing out that more has been given you, you cannot be justified in taking away the little which has been given him.[1]

The whole thinking world has reason to be grateful to Immanuel Kant for discovering and expressing a moral law of such universal application that, though it may always be supplemented, it is never likely to be outmoded. "So act," said Kant, "that thou dost treat every man, whether in thine own person or that of another, as always an end withal, and never as a means merely." This was Kant's second formulation of what he called the "categorical imperative," by which he meant a duty which is incumbent upon persons *absolutely*, rather than conditionally. There are some deeds which we ought to perform *if* we wish to accomplish certain ends, but which are not incumbent upon us under other circumstances and apart from these chosen ends. For example, if a person wishes to be a good runner, he must train, but apart from such an ambition he is under no such necessity. No doubt most moral imperatives are of this conditional variety, but there must be some which are

[1] *Letters and Speeches of Abraham Lincoln*, p. 98.

really unconditional. Are there, Kant asked, any moral positions which we ought to take, regardless? He found that the refusal to deal with men merely instrumentally was one such, and possibly the most important of which we can conceive.

Here we have, in this basic moral law, some hint of the possible richness of the objective moral order. The truth is that each person is *one* and that the good life between persons begins to appear when we treat men in the light of this fact. It is perfectly clear that each of us wishes to be so treated himself, since there are few experiences more shattering than to realize that the person whom we have trusted or helped has only been using us as a steppingstone to his own success, to be discarded when no longer needed. We know that such action is degrading. But other people are like ourselves in having their own unique individuality and consequent value. What is right in one instance is right in another of the same character. The outrage is to treat persons as things, to *use* them. Therefore we may restate the fundamental moral law as it concerns the relations between persons as follows: "Each person ought to treat all other persons as persons and not as things."

The reader will be quick to see that what we have just given is only another restatement of what is usually called the golden rule. This rule has sometimes been stated positively and sometimes negatively, but it received its classic expression among the ancient Israelites, as follows: "Thou shalt love thy neighbor as thyself." All of us know how we love ourselves. We desire our own genuine welfare; we hope to be treated as ends rather than means to other people's ends. Our duty is to seek this for all people, neglecting, for moral purposes, the distinction between *mine* and *thine*. Another way to say this is, that distinctions of mine and thine are morally irrelevant, no matter how important they may be for other reasons. We ought to seek the other person's welfare as vigorously as we seek our own. This is to apply to moral actions an objectivity like that applied in natural science. The scientist, as he observes phenomena, seeks to eliminate his own bias, his own prejudices, and, so far as is possible, his own subjective point of view. As scientist, he looks at his own body and, if possible, even at his own mind, with the same impartiality that he employs when looking at other bodies and minds. The essence of genuine morality lies in that complete impartiality which causes a man to refuse to make exceptions in his own case or judge his own actions by a standard different from that used in judging the actions of other men. The good man is neither easier nor harder on himself than he is on others. The central paradox is that, in following the principle of the supreme value of individual personality, we must, ourselves, be radically impersonal.

Herein lies the ultimate ground of our Western conception of even-handed justice, which is incredibly precious, even though we do not always illustrate it in practice. Because each individual is a center of value, we must be *impartial* in our treatment of all, and from this arises the twin concepts of due process and equality before the law. The legal ideal which the ethic of respect for persons entails is such that no particular characteristic of any man can be allowed to hinder a fair and impartial trial. We must see that the use of the courts to obtain redress is equally open to Negro and white, to Jew and Gentile, to Catholic and Protestant, to capitalist and communist, to rich and poor, to male and female, to learned and ignorant. We must be particularly careful to insure the civil liberties of those

who belong to unpopular groups, including those who deny
the validity of all Western ideals, even this one. The communist
may deny us equality of treatment on *his* principles, but we
must accord him equality of treatment on *ours*.

Imperfect as our practice is in following this ideal, we at
least hold it with sufficient clearness to make us a bit uncom-
fortable when we fail. Moreover we do often illustrate it in
remarkable ways, the most remarkable being that of the judicial
care given to the trial of communist leaders in the United
States. These men, accused of plotting the overthrow of the
government, were given opportunity to use all the devices of
delay and appeal that legal brains could contrive. The necessity
of scrupulous care on the part of a democracy, in dealing even
with subversive agencies, appears as a burden or handicap in
the race for world survival, but, in the long run, it may turn
out to be a source of incalculable strength.

We are all aware that what we call the race problem is one
of the most difficult which is faced by Western man. There is
no aspect of our life which makes us appear so hypocritical
and insincere as that according to which we force some of our
people into the status of second-class citizens, wholly on the
basis of race membership. But it is important to realize that
this is fundamentally a moral problem and one that cannot be
solved except by moral considerations. Racial equality is not
a doctrine which stands alone, but one which is a corollary
of the more fundamental thesis of respect for persons as persons. It is only as we become sincerely loyal to the primary
thesis that the race problem will even begin to be solved. What
is important to say, and to *mean*, is that the life we prize will
never be realized until men and women, regardless of color,

can enter places of *refreshment*, of *entertainment*, of *employment*, of *education* and of *worship*, without the nagging fear of being expelled or ignored. Until this is achieved, at least in great measure, we cannot expect the critics of our kind of life to take our high pretensions seriously.

It may perhaps be worth noting that this ethical position already outlined is not the same as *altruism*. The rule is not that we must love others *more* than ourselves or that we should love others only. We do have responsibilities to ourselves and the point is that, if we think reasonably rather than emotionally, we see that the responsibility to our own individuality and to the individuality of others is the same. Thus are transcended both egoism and altruism in what may be called ethical objectivism. Ethically speaking the distinction between "person" and "thing" is fundamental, but the distinction between "I" and "Thou" is incidental.

Such a moral principle may become, in countless concrete situations, a means of testing the rightness or wrongness of acts. The question always to ask of any act is, "What does it do to persons, including the person who performs it?" If there are acts which, by some social convention, have long been considered wrong in some particular society, and if, upon careful analysis, it is not possible to discover any way in which any persons are harmed by it, we must conclude that it is not wrong. Perhaps it is simply trivial, with little or no positive good, and in that event it does not belong to the moral realm at all. It is conceivable, of course, that any action in the world, no matter how trivial, would be recognized as having moral significance if we could see it in its total context and in the light of its total consequences, but, for practical purposes, many actions are rightly considered amoral.

The rule just suggested often has a wonderfully beneficent effect in liberating men and women from the bondage of conventional standards. Its application is almost sure to make them realize, not only the innocuousness of many deeds often disapproved by society, but also the wrongness of many deeds which society has generally approved. The method is no magic, but it brings a surprising amount of order into our popular ethical conceptions. The rule to the effect that the personal results are the criterion of moral worth will not give us quick and easy answers, as will an authoritative system, but it is like a compass in that it enables us to find the way for ourselves.

How difficult moral decisions are, and how inadquate even a rule as noble as the categorical imperative is, becomes clear when we consider a situation like the following. In 1914, a Belgian peasant, with his wife and children, was seeking to escape to France before the oncoming tide of war and was overtaken by a party of German cavalry. The Germans demanded certain information of a military character, but the peasant refused to supply it. Whereupon the officer in charge threatened that, unless the information was divulged, the man's wife and children would be lined up and shot. What was the man's duty? Would the categorical imperative help him there? We have to conclude that no single rule will suffice, though we do not doubt that there *is* a right action, however difficult it may be to discern. Our only safety lies in the continual increase of moral sensitivity, just as our best security in the judgment of beauty lies in the continual increase of aesthetic sensitivity.

There are many principles which we must honor and which apply to practical moral situations, but the sobering truth is, that the full application of one is frequently inconsistent with the full application of others. Thus it is certainly right to tell the truth, but it is also right to protect the innocent from suffering and torture. It is right to obey one's individual conscience, inadequate as it may be, since to fail to do so is to destroy integrity, but it is also right to maintain loyally the structure of the legal system which provides both order and protection. What does a good man do when the two conflict? The person who believes that there is some easy or simple answer to such questions is merely demonstrating his failure to understand the true complexity of the moral situation. We cannot solve such problems completely, but at least we can engage in thinking which narrows the area of perplexity. We are helped, for instance, by realizing that the ultimate reason for both honesty and promise-keeping is respect for persons whom dishonesty or broken promises will harm. In a world fundamentally impersonal there would be no valid reason for being careful about the truth, but in a personal world there is great reason to be careful, since dishonesty means taking advantage of the trust of others. The reason why it is wrong to break a treaty, by unilateral action, is that treaties are made with persons and the more fully the treaties have been motivated by trust, the greater is the potential harm in breaking them.

The danger of the strict moralist, whose main loyalty is to what he calls principles, is the danger of being brutal. We are familiar with the idealist whose devotion to a principle makes him bitterly censorious of those who do not seem to him to maintain this ideal and is sometimes impervious to the sufferings caused by the application of his principle. It is easy for a socialist, for example, to uphold strict socialist doctrine and be seemingly blind to the human suffering which his supposedly noble ideal entails. The reason why this is possible is that such a man believes that his chief loyalty is not to persons, but to precepts. He is concerned, as a modern thinker has phrased it, "not with living individuals, but with the abstract generalities of the moral law."[2]

A mark of the unbending moralist, who is concerned more with abstractions of the moral law than he is with persons, is that he has no real place in his system for forgiveness. How can there be room for forgiveness if it is *principles* that are precious? If the right is absolutely right, and therefore the same in all circumstances, it is surely as bad to excuse another as to excuse oneself. To excuse either oneself or another is to deny or neglect the universality of the moral law. It is from such hardness of heart that we are saved by an ethical system which makes respect for persons the central consideration. It does not, as we have shown, solve all problems, but it is the most promising start we know. *The noblest principle is that there is something more precious than principle.*

If it is important, on the one hand, to avoid the extreme of moral hardness, it is equally important to avoid the other extreme of sentimentality, especially that embodied in the adage that to understand all is to forgive all. The approach to moral problems which has been enunciated in this chapter is not at all the same as to say that all men are good or that evil men are never to be restrained. What such a principle rules out is not

[2] T. E. Jessup, *Law and Love*, p. 23.

restraint but *vengeance*. Cruel and wicked men must be imprisoned, not only in order to save innocent persons from their depredations, but also partly in the hope that the incarceration may help even the wicked men to become better men than they have been. However much we fail in practice, we at least pay lip service to this conception in the Western World by calling our houses of detention reformatories and penitentiaries, and, on some lives, they have the desired effect.

"Mankind," as John Stuart Mill said in a highly quotable phrase, "can hardly be too often reminded that there was once a man named Socrates." One of the startling ideas promulgated by Socrates in Athens in the fifth century B.C., was that it is never right to *harm* a man. No matter how evil he has been, said Socrates, you must never harm him, for then you make him *worse* and consequently add to the evil in the world, when it is your duty to detract from it. In our anger we may wish to punish a man, since, as we say, he has made others suffer and now he should suffer. It is conceivable that he ought to suffer if such suffering would open his eyes to what he has done and possibly advance him on the road to genuine penitence, but we cannot justify any other reason. Vengeance is wrong because it seeks the other person's *illfare*, whereas, if all personality is infinitely precious, we must always seek his *welfare*. To some this may seem an impossibly high ideal, but it is difficult to see how it is to be avoided if we follow the logic of the moral situation relentlessly.

It is obvious that we must often oppose evil men and their evil deeds resolutely and with all the appropriate means in our power, but we need a clear understanding of the ethical situation when we do so, for the very crusader against wrong is himself in danger. Our danger in opposing manifest evil is that, because by contrast we are indeed relatively less evil, we may come to think of ourselves as righteous. The temptation comes somewhat as follows:

> X is evil
> I am opposed to X
> Therefore, I am good.

But that which is opposed to evil is not, as a matter of fact, necessarily good, and may often be another form of evil, though perhaps a lesser evil. Our safety lies in the constant realization that all of us are men and that, as men, we are in the same fundamental predicament. One of the most penetrating of the ethical utterances of Aristotle is that to the effect that the alternative to an evil may not be a good, but merely another evil, for the simple reason that there are so many more ways of going wrong than there are of going right. "Evil actions," said Aristotle, "belong to the class of the infinite, but good actions belong to the class of the finite." When we aim at a target there is only one way of hitting it, but there are a million ways of missing it. Insofar as our reaction to the bitterness of our enemies is an equal bitterness we are merely demonstrating this ancient truth.

These considerations are highly relevant to the present world situation, which gives every appearance of continuing for many years. Ours is a world in which the relation to the avowed enemy is by no means a speculative or academic relation. What then shall our attitude be, if we are trying to learn to live as men ought, in our time of strain or any time of strain? We must stand firm against evil acts, but we must never let ourselves hate men, because hatred wounds the personality both of him who hates and of him who is hated. Since Socrates thought that people facing death often see through the confusion of existence with exceptional clarity we are wise to attend carefully to the words of Edith Cavell, just before she was shot by a German firing squad in October, 1915. Her words are part of the accumulated wisdom of mankind on how to live and how to die. "Standing as I do," she said, "in view of God and eternity I realize that patriotism is not enough. I must have no hatred or bitterness towards anyone."

VI

THE CLASSLESS SOCIETY

*Life has meaning only as one barters it day by day
for something other than itself.*
—ANTOINE DE SAINT EXUPÉRY

As we think seriously of our life in the West we are often critical of it, as we ought to be, because there are so many ways in which we fail to be loyal to our own basic dream, but we must never become so engrossed in this criticism that we fail to see the really remarkable achievements that have been made in the direction of a good life for all. We have some things in our life that are wonderfully worth keeping and that are illustrated in countless ordinary communities. Most of the readers of this book can point to the existence of hundreds or even thousands of towns and villages where there is a good life, both economically and spiritually, for the vast majority of the inhabitants. There are towns where scarcely a door is locked day or night, where there is often no policeman, and where the children of the banker and the children of the janitor attend the same school. Carpenter and judge meet as equals in the sight of God and both own the homes in which they live. Both have pride in the appearance of their homes and both improve the appearance of their streets by physical work on their lawns and gardens. Life's burdens and tragedies are shared, with no thought of class distinctions; there is vast generosity in case of illness; the children of both poor and rich go away to college;

and words such as "bourgeois" or "proletariat" are not even understood.

We take this situation so for granted that often we fail to realize how great a moral achievement it represents, how rich a social inheritance it is, and how sorely we should miss it if it were to be lost. We often fail to understand that these tremendous victories depend primarily, not upon material resources, but upon a particular world view, which is our most precious inheritance. It is only in certain centuries, and only in certain traditions, that so much good life for the common man has been possible.

In many ways the attitude toward work is central to the victories we have achieved and crucial to our further undertakings. For several centuries we have been developing, often tardily and always imperfectly, the idea that work is good, that it is something to be sought, and that work and ownership, far from being in any sense contradictory, go together as two parts of a single human pattern. It is in this mood that we have developed the wilderness, and produced our numerous industries. We have gloried in production and, though there have usually been monetary rewards, we have always understood that the work was good for its own sake, irrespective of its financial by-products.

It is in relation to work, so understood, that we see what may be the most serious threat to the life we have heretofore prized. We can go to pieces, either through the decay of the ideal of craftsmanship or through failure to respect the work we do. One of our greatest dangers lies in our education which takes many away from the learning of crafts at the very time when they might learn best, but fails to introduce them to any other area in which there is likelihood of their achieving a sense of competence. The few technical high schools we have are a mere gesture. The basic trouble lies not in our school system, but in our philosophy of work.

America, as is well known, is the West writ large. In this country we see both the evils and the virtues of Western civilization in exaggerated form, and we see, likewise, the tendencies which could, if allowed to grow, undermine the whole system. There is still a great deal of diversified ownership, as is demonstrated daily by the gigantic areas devoted to car parking adjacent to factories, and it is obvious that most factory workers do not desire any fundamental change in the system. It has been impossible, for the most part, for Marxism to get a serious foothold in the American labor movement and this chiefly for the reason that the men who work for wages are fully aware that they have a stake in a system of partially controlled enterprise which, in spite of its defects, seems to them to promise more for their families than can any alternative of which they are aware. There may, therefore, be little desire to change the system, but the danger is nevertheless great because so much of the attitude to the *work* itself is unsound.

The production line has been the means, more than any other single factor, of the present multiplication of manufactured goods, but we have had to pay a high price for this productivity. Perhaps the highest price we have paid is the loss of the ideal of craftsmanship in the thought of the average worker, who seldom has the satisfaction of making a finished product in its wholeness. What can the thrill of perfectionism mean to a man who works on the assembly line devoted to the making of refrigerators for persons he will never see and for whose admiration he cares not at all? Even if he wished to go back after hours to do extra work, he could not; he may live miles away and, besides, another man, belonging to the next shift, soon occupies his station. Naturally his eye is on the clock.

In our present situation the conventional opinion is that men work primarily for wages. Millions would not go near their places of employment if it were not for the necessity of earning bread. Since the satisfaction is seen wholly in the pay envelope and not at all in the work done, there is a continual drive for higher wages, which leads to higher prices and thus the spiral of inflation goes on. It is right that men should have a living wage, but it is never right that the earning of this should be the sole incentive to effort. When it is the sole incentive, the tendency is to do as little as possible, short of being fired. Accordingly there is strong pressure against the man who appears to be doing more than his fellows. Thus a premium is put upon mediocrity, excellence is frowned upon as antisocial and the result is a dull uniformity. The drive is constantly in the direction of less work, more pay and more idleness. If the leisure could be creative this situation might be a source of advance, but the unhealthy attitude to work tends to carry over into the unemployed hours.

Something of an index to wholeness of mind is to be found, as we have noted earlier, in the relative emphasis or lack of emphasis which men and women place on entertainment. When life is full and interesting, all we ask is more time to perform the tasks we have in hand. The consequence is that those who are living really satisfactory lives may go on for weeks without even the thought of consciously planned entertainment. But this fortunate situation is obviously rare in our contemporary society, since so many now make what is called recreation a steady and dominant interest. The amount of time, energy and money which goes into various forms of entertainment in the modern world is prodigious and, though accurate statistics are difficult to compile in this area, it appears that the total amount of money so spent surpasses the total amount spent on all education, both lower and higher. If, by some calamity of our own producing, our civilization should fall into sudden ruin and if, in later centuries, archaeologists were to dig among the ruins, they would surely be struck by the great number of outdoor theaters, each with its gigantic screen. The future archaeologist who knows little about us may even surmise, at first, that these screens are connected with some kind of re-ligious rite. If, by a religion, we mean that to which people really give themselves devotedly, he may not be utterly wrong.

The common feature of the greater part of our commercial entertainment, for which we willingly pay such phenomenal amounts, is that all point to *diversion*. The night club is de-signed to make the tired men and women who live in the city, or who are visiting the city, forget the labors of the day. Those who cannot afford such expensive diversion are given something which they *can* afford, and there are facilities for all. Those who stay at home can watch the television screen or listen to radio programs which, by means of artificial laughter, endlessly repeated, are designed to make people forget their burdens, their worries and their work. We may not be able to build and staff enough schools for all the children, but we have no shortage of race tracks. The magnitude and universality of such enterprises give a fairly accurate index of how lacking in satisfaction is the normal daily work. *The man who is not enthralled with his work, labors only for the money and then he must use a considerable portion of his money to secure the thrill which the work does not give.*

As we face this enormous and crucial problem we may as well be realistic about it and know, from the beginning, that we shall not turn the industrial clock back. The assembly line is here to stay and most of us are glad that it is. It is easy to become sentimental about an earlier age and to malign our own age unduly. Many of the products of an industrial society can help immensely, if rightly used, in making possible the good life for the majority of people. Whatever the critics may say about our plumbing culture, it is a good thing to be clean, and running hot water is a real boon, which we wish every person might enjoy.

We cannot base our moral philosophy for this century upon some fancied return to a simpler society, but must learn how, within the limits of the industrial society which we have, and shall continue to have, to keep open the creative springs for as many as possible. We need not suppose that the situation is hopeless. We must assume, as our ancestors have always done in hard situations, that there is a solution to our problem and that by taking thought we can make a difference. Our task is to try to change the climate of opinion, to build a different philosophy in men's minds, to teach a way of life. The fact that this task is long and difficult is no deterrent and is not even important.

There are a few basic principles which we have developed, tested and verified over the last two thousand years that can help greatly, not to change the system, but to enable men and women to live better within it. Since there is so little popular thinking on such matters that many are wholly unaware of even the existence of these principles, the effort to restate them may be productive.

The first principle in the philosophy of work is the principle of craftsmanship, the principle that happiness or well-being comes chiefly as a by-product of the performance of function in the way of excellence. This principle received its classic statement in the *Nicomachean Ethics* of Aristotle where it is the central theme, repeated many times with only slight variations. That the good life comes not by getting, but rather by *making,* is the most enduring ethical contribution of the famous Greek philosopher who was first to formulate the science of ethics.

Because man is so essentially the creator, he is never really satisfied unless he is, at some point in his life, engaged in creative work, and his best moments are usually those in which he is so engrossed in some kind of production that he forgets himself, his own ills and even the passage of time. If we live most fully in those moments when we are most forgetful of self, then we are happiest when we are engaged in some task which is within our powers, but makes severe demands upon our powers. The happy life is that in which we are accomplishing in a situation affording us scope, in the way of excellence, though often against great odds and with severe testing. Best of all is to produce something in the way of excellence that will outlast our mortal lives. "The great use of life," said William James, "is to spend it for something that will outlast it."

Men and women are made to do, to act, to create. Man is the worker, par excellence, who often supposes that he desires rest from toil, but whose actual joy comes in making a garden, a cathedral, a nation, a factory or a poem. The doing need not be physical doing, for much of the keenest joy lies in mental creation, as is vividly illustrated in the work of the scientist or the philosopher. Contemplation may be the most strenuous kind of doing and the most rewarding.

One of the chief reasons why the functional conception of human well-being is a sound one is that, by concentration upon the task, the doer achieves something like complete objectivity. The architect, who is striving to make a better plan for a new building, does not think constantly of *himself*, and this for the very good reason that the work of making the plan takes his entire attention. He does not have time to stop and admire his own skill or ask how he is progressing any more than the man who runs to report a fire in his own home stops to wonder about the quality of his running. Joy seems to come by concentrating on the object, whatever the object may be.

Almost everyone can remember some moments of real and true living. Are not these usually the moments of creation, no matter how modest? The writer, as he approaches the white paper of his unwritten book, hesitates to begin because the labor of verbal or logical construction is difficult and a thousand temptations for postponement come into the author's mind, but if he does really begin and the ideas begin to form themselves in a logical fashion, and the words begin to flow, the experience becomes amazingly rewarding. At the end of a morning of such work the writer looks back over the fleeting hours to realize that in this time he has truly lived. He has had some sense of being in his right place, of reaching his true home, of *belonging*. Such unfrustrated work, far from exhausting men, actually gives, in many lives, a sense of refreshment and renewal. What is tiring is interruption in work.

An essential part of this source of joy is the search for excellence, which is the desire for perfection. The life of artists often seems more enviable than that of others because, though ordinary life may have some of this, to the life of the artist it is central. The poet must often be tempted to let well enough alone, but, if he be a real poet, he is haunted by the vision of the perfect expression. In loyalty to this vision he struggles for the right word or the right music until he finds it. His life is not thereby made easy, since the vision drives him hard, but it is made glorious and then the fact that it is not easy is unimportant. How the violin player must be haunted by the possibility of an even more precise fingering! How the opera singer must struggle for perfect expression!

Nearly all persons admire the work of great singers or actors or writers or painters, but many seem to be unmindful, in their admiration or even envy, of the price which such persons pay. The struggle for excellence in any field is unremitting because men have to fight to retain heights, just as they fight to scale them. The price of excellence is unremitting toil, constant self-control and a continual disdain of the shoddy. But the persons who have followed this road, whatever the medium in which they have worked may be, are rightly recognized as the best that our race can show. They have not always been happy men and women in all their lives, for happiness is only one aspect of the good life, but the relevant fact is that they have had the vision of greatness, without which no moral progress is possible.

An important factor in the struggle for excellence in production is pride. Pride, in the sense of personal vanity, is often a blight on the human spirit, but there is a beneficent and wholesome pride which is pride in work accomplished. Part of the reason why the standard of performance in architecture is so high is that the architect knows very well that he will be judged by the finished building and that his particular work is of the kind which can never be hidden from public view. He cares, and ought to care, about his reputation, in the sense that he would be ashamed to be observed as doing slipshod work. This is the way Samuel Johnson felt about the production of his essays and poems. When asked once what the secret of his style was, he replied that he had early made it a habit to do his best on every occasion, whatever that occasion might be. He was a proud man, even in his poverty, and the world has profited by his pride.

Closely associated with such pride is professionalism. The idea of a profession is one that has contributed largely to our civilization in its best aspects and therefore one which we do well to cherish. A profession is a group of men and women who develop conscious standards of work to which they hold themselves and one another responsible. Nowhere is this more clearly beneficent than in medicine. The average citizen, who is terribly vulnerable in his relation to an inept or unscrupulous physician, is protected to some degree by legal arrangements, but the legal protection is only partial, since there are always ways in which laws can be circumvented. The patient's chief protection is the way in which doctors, through the centuries, have built up their own high standards and now bring strong pressure on one another to maintain these. We are saved from the poor doctor chiefly by his fellow doctors, who feel that in maintaining the code as represented by the oath of Hippocrates and by much more, they are part of something larger than themselves. They are, indeed, partners in a community of memory and of hope and the individual practitioner is kept from many practices simply by the thought that they are *unprofessional*. We take this feature of our civilization so for granted that we often fail to realize how precious it is and how hard it would be to develop if we did not have it. The experience of the production and growth of professional standards suggests that, in a truly good society, the real restraints must always be encouraged from *within* guilds of workers. The values of a profession come only by moral effort and cannot be enacted by law.

It is part of the condemnation of our age that most of us, while we give assent to Aristotle's principle and know that it is sound, feel that it has no relevance to the lives of the average workers in the twentieth century. But, unless we are willing to decay, we must *find* some relevance, so that the principle in question seems no longer remote. Actually we could promote the ideal of craftsmanship far more than we now do, if we really believed in it, in spite of our factory system. Part of our hope here lies in the fact that we have short hours of work and long weekends in which craftsmanship could be renewed, provided we were really in earnest. Modern industrialism, by the increase in production which makes possible the shortening of the working day, actually helps to provide its own antidote.

For millions in the modern world the major secret of creative work lies in the freedom, which almost all could have, to cut the day or the week into chapters. For those who hold the dullest jobs, without which our society cannot go on, this is a practical answer to the insistent problem of the discovery of some genuine significance in living. There are young men who work full shifts in factories and, at the same time, keep up full academic work leading to a degree. It may be argued, plausibly, that these young men do not get as much out of their college work as do those who have full time to give to it, but in any case their lives are far richer than they would be if they were to limit themselves to what, for most of their fellow workers, appears to be the only alternative, the factory shift and no more.

There are hard-working men who balance their lives admirably between work in an office, which they perform faithfully in order to feed themselves and their families, and work in a flower garden where their greatest effort is expended and where, consequently, their deepest satisfaction is found. These tend to be healthy-minded men. The weekend, which is so largely an invention of our time, is one of the potentially beneficent aspects of an economic system which, in so many other ways, is bad for men. It is hard to exaggerate the opportunity for balance in life which the long weekend provides for those able to take advantage of the situation. Great enterprises, such as home building, are sometimes completed by the cumulative use of this free time over many months and the by-products are as great as are the direct rewards.

We may be surprised to find how many opportunities there are for demonstrating the ideal of craftsmanship if we begin to look for them. Recently a lover of wood gave a college a load of cured wild cherry wood for the building of an extra large seminar table. At first it was difficult to find any workmen to undertake the job of constructing such a table, because it was largely a matter of hand work and original design. All expected such tables to be factory made. Finally two modest workmen undertook the job, made an attractive design that was not identical with any known pattern, and soon produced a table of exciting beauty. All of this was sure to be a source of satisfaction to generations of users of the table, but it was even more a source of satisfaction to the men who created the table. Their humble carpenter shop seemed to take on new dimensions as they worked. They did not stop to ask whether they were happy men, and certainly they had never heard of Aristotle's formula, but any observer could see how satisfactory their lives were. These craftsmen would have been surprised to hear it said, but actually they were aristocrats. Every man who works for the sake of work instead of reward is an aristocrat at heart.

It may be that millions are necessarily shut out from this kind of satisfaction by the very conditions without which an industrial system is impossible, but we must encourage every person to find the possibility of craftsmanship *somewhere* in his life. Only so can we rise to the stature of men rather than of machines. For some it may come in a new appreciation of the total significance of the work they are already doing; for others it may come in the development of hobbies in leisure hours; for still others it may come occasionally in vacations, when they can give their work away, as the people of Bali give their work on the construction of their temples. It is not easy for modern man to find such opportunities, but, if we are serious about the good life for all, we shall encourage this expectation and we shall help to provide opportunities. If we really cared about such matters, we might build some of our new structures by volunteer labor instead of always bowing down to the idol of the contract. That this is possible has been demonstrated recently in the construction of several fine buildings, one of which is actually being made by a combination of the efforts of organized labor, building contractors, unorganized paid workers and several hundred unpaid volunteer workers. We could duplicate such effort in other places if we really believed in the principle. Much of our failure now lies in the fact that we do not espouse the ideal. Our deepest tragedy, as mentioned earlier, is not the tragedy of failing to realize our dream, but that of not even having the dream.

Many who feel that they are in dull and uncreative work often envy others who seem to have marvelous opportunities. Opportunities do differ, but it is helpful to realize that no human task is wholly glamorous. When we see only the finished work it often seems wonderful, but no worth-while task is ever completed without passing through dull phases. Every profession includes humdrum work, which the person involved would gladly avoid if he could. Almost every job in the world involves features that are dull or unrewarding. The professor has endless student papers to read, the merchant has harassing books to keep and the mother has countless dull chores to do, especially when she is caring for little children. Anyone can stand some of this and ought to be glad to take his share, providing, at some point in his life, the chance to do the really creative task appears.

The other side of this truth is that no job is so dull and so mechanical that it denies, entirely, some creative outlet to the individual who is engaged in it. Even the person who works on the assembly line, handling the same interchangeable part every day, can reasonably feel some pride in the finished product which he and others have made possible, especially if it is a product which contributes to human welfare. Then, too, even those on the assembly line are side by side with other work-men, each of whom has his own problems, and it is not ab-solutely necessary that all conversation be meaningless or vapid. If the job is a routine one, which takes little concentration, and if it is dignified by the sense that it meets human needs, the worker is set free for what could be profitable thinking. The fact that such thinking is rare is no answer. We are con-cerned with what ought to be and with what *could* be.

"Moral progress is impossible," said the late Professor White-head in his most quotable aphorism, "apart from the habitual vision of greatness." Greatness is the stuff of morals and the enemy of all triviality. Some find the vision of greatness in the reading of Great Books or in the contemplation of great art and great ideas, but for the majority of men the vision of great-ness, if it comes at all, must come in connection with ordinary work and in the midst of ordinary life. It will come, not by any escape from the daily succession of ordinary experiences, but rather by a way of living which reveals the inherent greatness in common things. Any task, however humble, if it is under-taken in the desire to create excellence is thereby ennobled. In the long run that civilization will survive which is able to inspire its people with this ideal and to demonstrate it in the common round of daily duty.

A second relevant principle which bears directly on the problem of work, and which comes more from the Christian than from the Greek side of our heritage, is that involved in the idea of *vocation*. We frequently miss the significance of this word today, because it has been so widely used, but it has a rich history going back to the notion that every constructive task can be a divine calling. A man who tries to live his life in the spirit of vocation may perform any one of a thousand honest tasks, but, whichever one he performs, he begins with something akin to reverence because he knows he has only one life to live and he wants to make the best dent he can on this old world before he dies. He knows he may not have much to contribute, but he is in deep revulsion against the tendency to waste the little that he has. Such a person tries, often consciously, to match his individual powers against the world's need and thus discover what his true vocation is. It is obvious that a man who asks this question is very far from the man who asks the more conventional question of how he may advance himself socially or financially.

No person in his senses ever despises money, for money is an instrument of immense power. George Bernard Shaw was making an overstatement when he said[1] that money is the most important thing in the world, but we can agree that it *is* important because it will buy certain forms of human welfare. The only real value of money for any individual is that it will enable him to forward the interests about which he cares. Our time and energy are valuable for the same reason, and any person who acts upon this understanding is already beginning to know what vocation means.

One of the most revealing questions which a person can ever put to himself, and which we ought to put to ourselves periodically is: "What would I do with my time and energy

[1] In the preface to *Major Barbara*.

if I were suddenly, by some stroke of fortune, set free from the burden of earning my daily bread?" Some persons, undoubtedly, would go on doing precisely what they do now, but they are as rare as they are fortunate. They are the scientists who go back to the laboratory to potter around after the day's work is supposedly done; they are doctors who come home early from vacations. Often such men are working on some unsolved problem and it will not let them rest, but there is one problem such men seldom have, the problem of boredom. It is doubtful if most people have ever asked themselves this revealing question, but it might have startlingly beneficent effects if they were to do so. Though not all men can find work which is intrinsically satisfying, there is nothing wrong in as many as possible *trying* to find such work. A general revulsion against the work which is intrinsically unsatisfying or degrading or mechanizing to man is a wholesome revulsion and must always be encouraged.

We may as well face the fact that no human siutation is ever perfect. Every factory management has its difficult personnel, every office has its inner strife and contention, every university faculty has its academic feuds, every board of trustees has its members who hinder the action of others. This is the way the world is, and there is no other in which we have any present chance of working. The path of wisdom is to know that this is the case and to go forward gaily in spite of the drawbacks. What is desirable is the deep commitment in which a man decides to fight it out on a certain sector, for better and for worse. Such commitment is remarkably like that of marriage in which difficulties and dangers are faced in advance, but the commitment is meant to include and thus to supersede them. The commitment is big enough and inclusive enough to promise a steady affection "in sickness and in health" as well as "for richer and for poorer." Men and women achieve the greatest moral results from their work in the world when they approach their work in this mood.

There are, of course, positions in the world which are not really open to a man who seeks to live his life on a basis of vocation, because some jobs are parasitical, intrinsically trivial or even socially harmful. A man who finds himself in such a position, and who understands the idea of vocation, must have the courage to break out of his situation, whatever the personal price may be. There is a thrilling true story of an advertising man who has given up his job and taken work as a craftsman at one-fourth of his former income because, he said, he got tired of trying to make men drink one brand of whisky rather than another when he knew perfectly well that they were essentially the same. He is now a lucky man.

Any person who tries to live his life in the mood of vocation will always spend a great part of his time and energy in unmercenary labor. This ideal is what makes possible the enormous amount of time which busy men and women put into public service, which is so intrinsic a part of the life we prize that we are almost unaware of it. Though some of the avenues of human service are now largely given over to the government, our tradition is still that of a phenomenal amount of private giving in the support of hospitals, colleges, and all kinds of privately financed public work. This is more precious than we know.

One of the noblest aspects of the vocation ideal is the expectation that men may live their lives in chapters, often

giving the last big chapter to wholly unmercenary labor. Thus
the principle of alternation, so often applied to small units of
time within the day or within the week, may be applied even
more to large segments of an entire career. The scholar who
has spent ten years in work of a theoretical nature may give
the next ten years to the effort to apply his theory to concrete
situations. At the end of such a period he might profitably
give his time to some third interest and so on until he dies. It
is, of course, frustrating to try to do several things at once,
but we can live our lives serially, if we will, and the consequent
richness is often amazing. The modern world has seen many
brilliant illustrations of this way of life, one of the finest being
in the career of Ray Lyman Wilbur, who was first family
physician, then professor, then university president, then statesman, then university president again and finally, after retirement, wise counselor to numerous persons engaged in various
types of public service.

If we had enough imagination we should realize that such
a pattern need not be limited to a giant like Dr. Wilbur, but
might, in some measure, be the regularly expected pattern in the
lives of countless humble citizens. Not all could follow it, but
it could be much more widely extended than it now is. The
chief deterrent is not a lack of financial resources or a lack of
opportunity, but simply a failure of imagination or understanding of the idea.

With so much to be done in the world it is often a shame
for a person to have only one career when he might have
several. Why should not a successful businessman end his business career long before he is tired out and give the rest of his
days to scholarship, to public service, to some profession? Nor-

mally we fail to do this, not because it is essentially impracticable, but because it does not occur to us, but, if we should take the notion of vocation seriously, it *would* occur to us.

There is something wonderfully refreshing about the example of the schoolteacher who retired at sixty-five, started at once to law school, and is now practicing law in his seventies. Why not? Life is so rich in its possibilities that it is a shame to miss all of them except one. Human life is sufficiently long that it can profitably be lived in chapters and each chapter be really significant. An encouraging illustration of such a life is seen in the career of the late Lord Tweedsmuir, whose autobiography is much admired on both sides of the Atlantic. The young John Buchan felt in himself many different powers and he developed several of them by the simple expedient of developing them one at a time. He was a soldier, author, businessman and statesman and yet his life had an underlying unity. There were different chapters, but all were chapters in the same book.

No group in the world are more free to apply this principle of creativity than are women. Most women become mothers and accordingly are fully employed for several years with inescapable tasks. These tasks, which are sometimes too heavy, suddenly and inevitably come to an end. The change which comes in a woman's life when the youngest child achieves relative independence is really a revolution. The part of wisdom would be to look upon this revolutionary change as an opportunity to embark on new pursuits, which might give chances for the creation of unsuspected forms of excellence. Because we do not believe this, and thus make the expectation general, countless women become a burden to themselves and others, frustrated because they do not know how to occupy the suddenly acquired free time. The change that could come in civilization if this vast human resource were creatively used to full capacity is incalculable, but we shall never take anything like full advantage of it until the concept of vocation is better understood, better disseminated and consequently more generally accepted.

The recognition of the validity of the idea of vocation would help countless women at both ends of their mature existence. During the early years of married life there is obviously a strong temptation to escape from the heavy responsibilities of child care, a temptation to which many succumb with serious consequences in the lives of children. The notion that a woman can have two full-time careers is a thoroughly exploded one and most thoughtful people are beginning to realize that motherhood itself is a full-time career, demanding all the intelligence that any person can muster. The woman who accepts her responsibilities loyally will bravely restrict her outside activities at one period, but will accentuate them at another. Part of the incidence of mental illness among married women undoubtedly arises because this principle is not understood.

A third relevant principle, which has been late in its full development, though its roots are found in the ancient culture, particularly the Hebrew, is that of *ownership*. Perhaps the basic story is the story of Naboth's vineyard, the chief point of which is that even the royal house had no right to dislodge the humble man from his own acres, which constituted his family inheritance. The idea is that ownership is good, and that, consequently, we ought to extend it to as many people as possible. Ownership is good, not because things are more precious than persons, but because ownership, under proper circumstances and with proper limitations, dignifies and ennobles the lives of the persons concerned. It is part of our task, in developing the philosophy of the life we prize, to try to know which particular limitations are the proper ones.

The Russians, as is well known, do not accept this principle as valid. They believe that it is wrong (1) to engage in trade and (2) to employ labor. In their system, as a compromise, they have permitted certain minor forms of personal ownership, but in their view, these are necessarily severely limited because ownership in general is not prized. On the other hand, we have prized it very much. It is one of the aspects of our system, which others find hard to understand, that great numbers of our industrial workers not only own their homes and the cars in which they ride to work, but also own stock in the very companies by which they are employed. Millions of our workers are thus capitalists, as many of our capitalists are workers. This is why words like "bourgeois" and proletariat" seem to us to have so little relevance.

Our Western ideal has been symbolized, in a magnificent way, by *the man who works the land he owns.* He is neither the absentee landlord nor the peasant nor the peon, but a proud man who, by means of a mortgage, buys a one-hundred-sixty-acre farm, and works hard on it all his days. He is a dirt farmer, but, in thousands of cases, he sends his children to college, takes an important part in government and lives a life as full of dignity as of hard labor. Sometimes we forget how remarkable this type is, but such a pattern is really a great human achievement for which we have reason to be grateful. It has not been possible to produce this in most parts of the world and will not always be possible in the heart of the West, unless we give the pattern wise and loving care.

This combination of work and ownership, which has been our glory, could easily be lost and has already been lost in some parts of the West. It is lost whenever the men and women who do the hard work come to look upon themselves as mere employees, without a stake in the enterprise. Big agriculture may be as great a social danger as is big industry.

The beneficence of ownership is seen vividly in the effect which home ownership normally has on children. Children, to grow up well, need a sense of belonging. To be always in the house which belongs to someone else, or always to use another's furniture, may be really damaging to young minds. Children need a sense of permanence with a base where they have a perfect right to be, and that is what ownership means.

If we begin to understand the significance of this principle we see what is wrong with the concentration of wealth in a few hands. Concentration of wealth is evil, not because wealth is evil, but because it is good. It is so good that we ought to produce a system in which all who are willing to *work* will be able to *own*. If anything is good it ought to be distributed as widely as possible.

Our Western ideal, to which we are already partly disloyal, and which we are always in danger of losing, is really that of the classless society. We reject, on the one hand, the caricature of capitalism, in which a few own and the many work with no enduring stake in the community. We reject, on the other hand, the caricature of socialism in which no individual owns, but all belongs to that abstraction called the state. What we espouse is the pattern of life according to which every person works, with hand or brain, in which there are no parasites, and likewise in which all have a stake in the total wealth in what is called private ownership. We have not achieved this ideal, but it is the fairest we know and, whatever progress we have made thus far, has come by our approximation to it.

VII

THE BASIS OF INTEGRITY

*The love of praise-worthiness is by no means derived
altogether from the love of praise.*

—ADAM SMITH

Man is a creature who is concerned with his own standing in
the opinion of his fellows. The pain that can be given by general neglect or by general contempt is far harder to bear than
is most physical pain and lasts far longer. As human self-consciousness has developed it has been marked by very strong
desires, the desire for good reputation in the eyes of others
being one of the strongest of these. The basis on which reputation rests may differ markedly as between nations and tribes,
but so far as we know, there is no people without it.

The deep desire for human approbation is, so far as we can
see, a necessary element in the production of what we normally
call civilization. Civilization is maintained, at all levels, by a
host of intangibles and, among them, the desire for reputation
is apparently one of the chief. Men are often kept from running
from the scene of danger, not because there is any physical
hand restraining them, but because they would be called cowards if they were to run away, and because they care what
their fellows think about their character. Safety, a full meal
and a warm fire might be enough for "peace of body," but man
is so made that he requires far more than these for his full satisfaction. Indeed, the sense of general approbation makes it pos-

sible for men to endure terrible physical hardship over long periods.

The power of the desire for approbation may be illustrated in many striking ways. One is the fact that ostracism, especially noncommunication while the offending person remains physically present, has long been considered one of the worst of punishments for alleged wrongdoing or for failure to be in harmony with the wishes and opinions of the group. Another illustration is the way in which we have an interest in even posthumous reputation, though we are fully cognizant that we shall not be present to enjoy it. The present satisfaction in contemplating a situation in which our action is approved at some future date is so great that it is sufficient to overcome any sadness at the thought of our absence from the happy scene. The way in which numerous prominent men are careful to preserve every scrap of evidence about their actions, especially on those points where they have been criticized and where the evidence seems to justify their actions, tells us a great deal about human nature. Approbation is felt by us to be so good that it transcends even the limits of time and of mortality.

That this basic desire for social approval has numerous beneficent effects we cannot doubt. It enforces actions for the welfare of the group that mere law or police power could never enforce. Plato uses effectively the story of the ring of Gyges which had the magic quality, when the signet was turned inward, of rendering the wearer invisible, and the reader of *The Republic* is bound to ask himself how different his actions would be, were he the possessor of the legendary ring. Even relatively decent people are frequently kept from performing slightly shady acts by the fear of possible disclosure and consequent loss of reputation in the minds of people about whose opinions they care. The punishment of a fine or even imprisonment is often trivial in comparison with the punishment involved in newspaper publicity of a damaging character. Consequently, the actual imprisonment of a man in public life, at the end of a trial, is relatively unimportant, since his real punishment has already occurred. This is why the spread of gossip in undermining a man's reputation is so effective and also so cowardly. Even when the gossip is fought openly it has already done some of its deadly harm, since many people will say wisely to their neighbors, "Where there is so much smoke there must be some fire."

We realize more clearly the power involved in the desire for approbation when, by some change in circumstances, its hold on men and women is lessened. This is often seen when a person from a small community moves into an urban setting, in which there are none of his former companions. Frequently he becomes a radically different person, in both his actions and his standards of moral judgment, largely because he is no longer subject to the same social pressures. He is uprooted from the old setting; he is free from its restraints, because his actions are no longer observed and judged by the same people about whose opinion he has always cared. Thus character and reputation are deeply intertwined, and the person in question is essentially two persons because of the two groups whose approval he prizes. Returning to his rural or village home, the man who has settled in the city often takes on his former character again. On the whole, an uprooted character deteriorates unless it finds some other group to which it can be united so that a new set of desires for approbation are effective in conduct.

Valuable as this desire for good reputation may be, and necessary as it is to the maintenance of any civilization at all, we are bound to realize that it is also one of the most dangerous forces in human life. Like most sources of power it can be directed to harm as well as to gain and, without wise attention, inevitably becomes harmful. Whenever the desire for popularity becomes an end directly sought, so that it is the center of consciousness rather than a mere deterrent to irregular action, it can destroy both peace and happiness as well as character. What may ordinarily be a normal part of social structure becomes an obsession. Then those so obsessed are always trying to look two ways at once, one eye being centered on the task to be done and the other directed to the effect on the minds of others in either praise or blame.

The desire for popularity, which may so easily become overweening, can never bring steady satisfaction to any person, and is, in fact, a symptom of emotional insecurity. It is because we are not really sure about the worthiness of our conduct that we seek so desperately the buttressing effect of what others may say. We seek the approval of others, as Adam Smith said, because "their approbation necessarily confirms our own self-approbation."[1] The desire for popularity is unsatisfying, in the first place, because the appetite grows as it is fed, so that the demand is always for more and more. The man of power surrounds himself with admirers, but they must always be *more* admiring, with the consequence that those who fail to keep pace are regularly replaced by others of greater promise in this regard.

The philosopher Thomas Hobbes is not remembered for

[1] Adam Smith, *The Theory of the Moral Sentiments*, III, ii.

much that is good, but he is remembered for his near-perfect account of the way in which the love of power over others is never satisfied. It is never satisfied, said Hobbes, because the *present* power cannot be retained unless it is increased. The relevant passage from *The Leviathan* is as follows:

I put for a general inclination of all mankind, a perpetual and restless desire of power after power, that ceaseth only in death. And the cause of this is not always that a man hopes for a more intensive delight than he has already attained to, or that he cannot be content with a moderate power; but because he cannot assure the power and means to live well which be both present, without the acquisition of more.[2]

The point to make is that an appetite that grows constantly in its demands and is never satisfied is really a source more of pain than of joy. Readers of Plutarch will remember the bitter ending of the life of Caius Marius, the classic example of the bitterness which can be engendered by unrestrained ambition. The thirst for adulation and power became so feverish that Marius ended his days, says Plutarch, in virtual madness, though he was the first man to be made Consul of Rome seven times.

In the second place popularity is, in the nature of the case, bound to change. Fame, as the ancients have told us, was always a fickle goddess and the people who shout acclaim today may be shouting denunciations tomorrow. The person who counts heavily on praise will necessarily be equally affected by blame. If popular acclaim is the chief good there is no escape from the conclusion that popular denunciation is the chief evil.

There is no doubt that cruel criticism is one of the heaviest burdens which those who try to accomplish anything in the

[2] Thomas Hobbes, *The Leviathan*, Chap. XI.

world have to bear. The person who tries to achieve any kind of excellence will inevitably be criticized for trying to be high and mighty, because mediocrity always resents excellence and accordingly seeks to attack it. The reason for the attack is that the very existence of excellence is a standing criticism of the mediocrity itself. In similar fashion the person who loyally accepts responsibility for a cause is sure to be criticized for being dominating or aggressive. Anyone who puts his head above the heads of the crowd is thereby inviting the censure of all the envious. So great is this burden that it becomes a real deterrent to some tender minds and it is, no doubt, an incentive to millions to remain in safe anonymity.

The only security in these matters lies in a certain imperviousness to both praise and blame. It does no good to try to close our ears to the harsh criticism and then try to listen eagerly to the sweet strains of popular adoration. The patent inconsistency of this situation renders it untenable for a rational mind. It is only when we are relatively impervious to praise that we are strong enough to be equally impervious to blame. But the man who maneuvers for compliments and praise, putting his back in a position to be easily patted, is thereby rendering himself vulnerable. The great Doctor Johnson understood this so well that, in one of his finest prayers, he asked that neither praise would fill him with pride, nor censure with discontent.

The secret of such a position of imperviousness to criticism lies in the very objectivity already mentioned more than once in this volume. The person who can so fasten his attention on the job to be accomplished that the work takes all of his attention and interest, has *for that reason*, no attention left for what people may say. Then he can reply, when the grumblings

come, thick and fast, "They say; let them say!" Few men have
even been able to demonstrate this more perfectly than Abraham Lincoln, in the last four years of his amazing life. He
realized that he had many enemies, many critics and many
slanderers, but he had practically no time to consider them
because all of his energy was directed to a single end, the saving
of the Union. He had learned early the foolishness of nursing
insults or harboring grudges, because he observed that persons
who remembered personal injuries succeeded only in injuring
themselves the more. Once, when an attack was being made on
the President by the Committee on the Conduct of the War,
because of one of his "blunders," and he was talking with an
officer who possessed official evidence that showed the Committee's criticism to be completely unfounded, the officer
asked, "Might it not be well for me to set this matter right in
a letter to some paper, stating the facts as they actually tran-
spired?" "Oh, no," replied the President, "at least not now. If
I were to try to read, much less answer, all the attacks made
on me, this shop might as well be closed for any other business.
I do the very best I know how—the very best I can; and I mean
to keep doing so until the end. If the end brings me out all
right, what is said against me won't amount to anything. If the
end brings me out wrong, ten angels swearing I was right
would make no difference."

We are now so accustomed, in all parts of America, and in
most parts of the Western World, to the recognition of Lincoln
as a man of stature, perhaps the man of the greatest moral
stature which the nineteenth century produced, that we tend
to forget the bitterness of the constant attacks upon him when
he was bending every effort toward a great end. One of the

noblest poems ever printed in *Punch* was one in which, in the spring of 1865, that magazine made public penance for its ignoble jibes about a noble man. Almost daily, during his administration, President Lincoln could have read, if he had wished to take the trouble, bitter and intemperate attacks upon himself, his intelligence, his appearance, his very character. As late as June 9, 1864, less than a year before Lincoln's assassination, the *New York World* published:

The age of statesmen is gone, the age of rail-splitters and tailors, of buffoons, boors and fanatics, has succeeded. . . . In a crisis of the most appalling magnitude, the country is asked to consider the claims of two ignorant, boorish, third-rate backwoods lawyers, for the highest stations in the government. . . . God save the Republic!

There was no better indication of the greatness of Lincoln than the fact that he did not bother to reply. If he had replied he would have been conducting the struggle on the level where his opponents were operating. Persons at all levels of public life can profit enormously by this example and follow the two-fold creed which Lincoln and others have demonstrated. The first item is to act with such complete honesty that one is not secretly ashamed, and the second is to neglect, in large measure, what people say. A contemporary college president, asked how he had been able to keep his composure in the face of continual shots fired at him from students, from professors, from alumni and from the general public, replied, with a broad and genuine smile, "Oh, I just keep moving and let the shots drop behind me."

When, at Appomattox, General Robert E. Lee had determined upon surrender, because he saw that continued fighting would destroy many lives without accomplishing any good end, one of his officers remonstrated saying, "Oh, General, what will history say of the surrender of the army in the field?"

"Yes," replied the sober Lee, "I know they will say hard things of us! They will not understand how we were overwhelmed by numbers. But that is not the question, Colonel: The question is, is it right to surrender this army? If it is right, then I will take all the responsibility."[3]

It is obvious that a man, acting as Lee acted, has already found a deep peace, even though personal peace is not what such men seek. Their deepest secret is a certain humility in that they understand accurately the littleness of their own lives and realize that the fate of mankind is of vastly more importance than the fate of their own reputations. After the war in which General Lee fought so long was over and he was already the legendary hero of his people, a young mother came to him with her baby, seeking a blessing. Lee took the little one in his arms, looked at it, looked at her, and then said slowly, "Teach him he must deny himself."[4]

We cannot, of course, neglect all criticism of our productions and we ought not to neglect all. There are times when we can be thankful for criticism because it helps us to avoid conceit and makes us conscious of our essential smallness. In one of the *Little Flowers*, St. Francis of Assisi expresses himself as being able to bear the attacks of harsh opponents who say terrible things, by reminding himself "humbly and charitably" that the critic knows him truly.

Though all moral philosophers have laid stress on the re-

[3] Carl Sandburg, *Storm Over the Land*, p. 227.
[4] *Ibid.*, p. 242.

sponsibilities we owe to one another, and rightly so, there is a sense in which each person must be loyal to his own dream of a unified life for himself. The following of such a dream, whatever others may say or fail to say, is a great part of what we mean by integrity and a means to satisfaction on a high level. Since it is frustration that lies at the root of most unhappiness, the path to a really satisfying life lies through the achievement of unity of aim and purpose, which permits no deviations such as may be dictated by those who would seek to divert. There is an old story to the effect that once a traveler in ancient Greece had lost his way and, seeking to find it, asked directions of a man by the roadside, who turned out to be Socrates. "How can I reach Mt. Olympus?" asked the traveler. To this Socrates is said to have replied gravely, "Just make every step you take go in that direction." A man who can keep his eye on his goal and not waste undue time or energy in answering critics is well on the way to his own Mt. Olympus, however modest his particular peak may be. To a great extent what we call integrity comes by singleness of purpose as against confusing claims, and the greatest enemy of such singleness is extreme sensitivity to criticism. The creed of a beneficent individualism has seldom been better stated than in the following words of Woodrow Wilson:[5]

Where the individual should be indomitable is in the choice of direction, saying: "I will not bow down to the weak habit of pursuing everything that is popular, everything that belongs to the society to which I belong. I will insist on telling that society, if I think it so, that in certain fundamental principles it is wrong; but I won't be fool enough to insist that it adopt

[5] Ray Stannard Baker, *The Public Papers of Woodrow Wilson*, Vol. II, pp. 185, 186.

my programme at once for putting it right. What I do insist upon is speaking the full truth to it and never letting it forget the truth; speaking the truth again and again and again with every variation of the theme, until men will wake some morning and the theme will sound familiar, and they will say, "Well, after all, is it not so?" That is what I mean by the indomitable individual. Not the defiant individual, not the impractical individual, but the individual who does try, and cannot be shamed, and cannot be silenced; who tries to observe the fair manner of just speech but who will not hold his tongue.

The paradox is that a man such as Wilson sought to describe in this passage, and which he obviously sought to be in his own life, becomes an individual precisely because he minimizes his own importance. He cannot be shamed and cannot be silenced, because he recognizes that what happens to him is not really of great moment, whereas what happens to the cause which he serves is tremendously important. The way out of the perils of the desire for approbation is not to be wholly insensitive to its claims, but to transcend it in the light of a larger claim. The only man who can rightly be impervious to his personal reputation is not the man who fails to *care*, but the man who cares supremely. He cares for something so much that the problem of his own reputation becomes, in comparison, an insignificant detail.

This sense of personal integrity combines easily with great restraint in the criticism of others. It is sheer sentimentality to suppose that we must never criticize or engage in moral judgment, for a world in which everything is considered lovely is essentially the same as one in which nothing is lovely, but this sentimentality is not the primary danger most moderns face. Our danger, by contrast, is that of being bitterly censorious of the acts of others, often wounding tender people very deeply, including those who do most for us in public life. One of the best antidotes to the habit of censoriousness is the keen recognition of our own faults and failures. Most of us fail too often in our own lives to be able, with any convincing quality, to make harsh judgments of our neighbors. In any case a good man will always seek to err, if he errs at all, on the side of sternness in judging his own conduct and on the side of tenderness in judging the conduct of his fellows.

The basis of integrity consists, as the great Adam Smith saw so clearly, in the ability to transcend the concept of praise and concern ourselves with the concept of praiseworthiness. The point is that similarity between these is delusive, since they belong to different orders of thought. Man is a creature who can ask of an action, not merely "Will it be praised?" but "Ought it be?" and no amount of affirmative answers to the first question can balance a negative answer to the second. What helps us is not so much to ask what our contemporaries think and not even what succeeding generations will think, but what would be the judgment of an impartial observer who could see the action in its entirety? This may seem very high ground, but it is central to the moral tradition of the West, which is now in jeopardy from so many directions. It may be high ground, but when catastrophe threatens it is reasonable to ask whether survival is possible on any other.

This philosophy has a direct bearing, not only on the life of individual men, but also on the life of nations, and is especially relevant in contemporary America. As a nation we have come into a time when we are harshly and often unjustly criticized. Naturally, we care. We do not easily forget that our casualties have been many while the casualties of our severest critics have been few. We see no reason to respect the position of those who, though agreeing equally to the fundamental decision of 1950, have not only failed to bear an equal burden in implementing it, but have also engaged in cruel criticism of those who do bear the burden.

It cannot be denied that this situation is an unhappy one and, in spite of our mistakes, one that is relatively unjust. But the path of wisdom lies clearly in the neglect of whatever criticism is merely censorious. We have come, as a nation, into a situation of almost overwhelming responsibility in the modern world and we dare not let our course be deflected by the desire for popularity or greatly bothered when unpopularity comes. A truism *may* be true, and the ancient moral wisdom is that our task, as a people, is not the task of winning popular approval, but rather of finding the right course and following it single-mindedly and loyally.

VIII

THE NECESSITY OF BOLDNESS

Yes, but you must wager. It is not optional. You are embarked. Which will you choose then?
—BLAISE PASCAL

When the ancient Greek thinkers analyzed human conduct, distinguishing the right from the merely prudent, they finally arrived at substantial agreement that the ultimate virtues were four: wisdom, courage, temperance and justice. We have inherited this analysis in the Western world so that our total moral picture has involved these cardinal virtues, along with additional ones, particularly those stemming from Palestine.

The ideal of justice, supplemented by the respect for persons as persons, which stems chiefly from the other main source of our Western tradition, has been profoundly influential in the development of our moral ideal and in the consequent criticism of our practice, but the ideal of courage has been almost equally so. Most readers respond sympathetically to the words of the rustic with which Hugh Walpole begins his book *Fortitude*, " 'Tisn't life that counts; it's the courage you bring to it." The difference between life and the good life is immense, and there are certain ways in which we have learned that the good life comes. There are some men and women who seem to live above or beyond the frustration which is so common a feature of our contemporary society, and, more often than not, these unfrustrated souls are people who live with conspicuous and unhesitating boldness.

There is, of course, no magic recipe for the good life, but we can learn much from those who, by common consent, have lived well, and the great majority of such persons have been men and women of outstanding boldness. They may seek at first to make sure that they have considered as many of the relevant factors in the situation as can be known, but they do not forever balance the factors against each other, nor, once the choice is made, do they spend time and mental energy in futile anxiety as to whether the decision was the right one.

Tentativeness, all agree, is good up to a certain point and in certain areas of experience. There is a sense in which every hypothesis is tentative, because there is always the possibility that another hypothesis will appear which will account for the facts more completely, but even in scientific method the time must come when one alternative is boldly accepted and tried. Indeed it is doubtful if truth is ever verified in any other way. Thus Columbus, in order to test his theory, had to believe in it enough to risk his reputation and his own life, as well as the lives of his comrades, in order to prove its truth. The great forward steps in human knowledge come not primarily by the work of those who stand off in splendid detachment, but far more by those who are bold enough to commit themselves to a position.

The fruitfulness of such decision may be illustrated in many biographies, ancient and modern, for biography is, indeed, the raw material of ethics. One modern illustration, vivid to the author by personal contact, is seen in the life of the late Ray Lyman Wilbur, who, as his loyal colleagues either in govern-

ment or university experience will testify, exhibited this characteristic to a marked degree. A long-time colleague has stated
the matter thus:

One of his striking attributes was his ability to reach a
decision, sharp and clear, if the facts were at hand, with amazing swiftness. A caller at his office on some troublesome question often found that, even before he had fully stated the case,
the smiling president had picked out the issue, diagnosed it
clearly, and was ready with the answer. There had been no
lengthy exchange of views, no wrinkling of brows.[1]

It may be said that intellectual decisiveness of this character
depends on great mental powers, such as Dr. Wilbur undoubtedly possessed. Perhaps so, but at least we can be sure that such
mental powers, of themselves alone, are not enough for this
phenomenon; they are not a sufficient condition. What may be
even more important as a necessary condition is the conscious
development of a *habit of decision*. This not only gets much
more accomplished in the world than can be accomplished
without it, but also brings a marked sense of peace to the person
who demonstrates it. Such a person knows very well that he
may turn out to be wrong in some of his decisions, but he also
knows that life is full of forced options and there is no safety
in refusing to decide. To refuse to decide is often in itself a
decision and sometimes an irrevocable one. If I refuse to decide
whether I shall let the weeds of my garden go to seed, I am
already deciding.

An unforgettable illustration of a forced option is President
Truman's decision, in the early summer of 1950, concerning the
defense of South Korea, for which, under the United Nations,

[1] Robert E. Swain, "Ray Lyman Wilbur: 1875-1949." *Science,* March
31, 1950, pp. 324-27.

the American government felt temporarily responsible. Part of the world still applauds his decision as a rare and responsible act of courage, while another part of the world condemns it as "aggression," and still another part believes, on prudential grounds, that the wrong decision was made. It is easy to criticize now, but the relevant fact to keep in mind is the inevitability of the decision *then*. The President could, of course, have postponed a decision because of the difficulty of the situation, but such a postponement would, of itself, have been a decision in another way. What is inescapable in our finite existence is that decisions have to be made *before* the full evidence of success or failure is available, and it is altogether too easy to seem wise after the event.

Though this illustration is particularly compelling because the issues involved are of such great importance to so many people, it is only in degree that this situation differs from other moral situations which face common men and women every day in every walk of life. We tend to suppose that we can postpone all action, unmindful of the fact that such postponement is itself a sort of action. The forced option is more common than we realize.

There is, then, in the good life, something of the element of the gambler's art. The gambler is one who not only believes in one outcome rather than another, but also one who is willing to prove his belief by staking something on it. In games of mere chance this demands no intellectual effort and becomes a stupid vice, while in the case of sufficient bribery, the element of chance is removed, and it becomes merely a crooked business, but in affairs of common life the true wager is often a virtue. It is, of course, in most instances far easier to sit back and refuse to take a stand, partly because such action seldom looks ridiculous. We hate to be laughed at, to look the fool, and the easy way to avoid this role is to maintain the position of indifference. Then no one can validly say, "I told you so." When nothing is staked nothing can be lost, but it is likewise true that little is ever accomplished.

There is no doubt that much of our popular philosophy points us in the direction of safe indifference on all issues. This philosophy is expressed in popular slogans, such as "Don't stick your neck out" and "Don't go out on a limb." The modish thing is keep cool, to avoid getting hot and bothered, to look with interest, but not involvement, at the current scene. Such a philosophy is easy to understand, but it can never be really admired because it is based on the fear of seeming foolish or on the fear of being proved wrong. In short, it is based on cowardice.

Safe as such moral prudence may be, the person who espouses it is necessarily shut out from most of life's great moments. The person who never goes out on a limb will never, it is true, have the limb cut off while he is on it, but neither will he reach the best fruit. The best fruit which human life offers seems to come only within the reach of those who face life both boldly and gaily, and with no excessive concern over possible failure or personal danger. The good life is always the gambler's choice, and comes to those who take sides. Neutrality is seldom a virtue.

We have been taught, in our time, the intellectual virtue of being sure that we see all the evidence, on both sides. This is indeed a virtue, but we make a terrible mistake when we suppose that it is the only one. The balanced judgment is only the beginning and before it can reach fulfillment, must be followed by the leap of faith which is courageous commitment. Such commitment need never be the blindness of credulity. It is not and ought never to be "belief in spite of evidence," but it must be "life in scorn of consequences," especially when we are referring to consequences to ourselves. Such a life may have something of the gaiety of a little child whose view of the future is too slight to provide a real basis for anxiety. This may be part of the meaning of the revolutionary saying, "Except ye become as a little child, ye cannot enter in."

Such gay and bold lives may often do the world far more good than is done by the deadly serious people. As we think of those who have helped us most, we usually realize that we have been helped enormously by persons who have had no idea that they were helping, and who helped chiefly by the simple fact that they were gay. We do not always remember with pleasure those who have performed conscious services to us, even though we may be grateful to them, but we do remember with pleasure those people whose daily gaiety has been infectious. This is only another form of the moral truth that we serve more by what we *are* than by what we *do*.

The moral necessity of facing life as a continuous wager is clearly demonstrated in the decisions of common life, as is seen vividly in the momentous enterprise of starting a home. It is doubtful if any person would ever start on the amazing venture of establishing a family if he could see in advance all the problems, all the dangers and all the toils that are involved. How can I know, beyond a shadow of doubt, that this woman whom I take as the life of my life will always be attractive, always loving, always co-operative? The answer is that I cannot know. My great venture, the most important I shall ever make, may turn out to be a failure, but I cannot hedge my bet. If I try to do that, seeking to play safe by making the arrangement merely temporary or tentative, then I destroy almost surely any chance of real success and I debase the entire undertaking. The wager itself is the greatest single factor in making success possible. Because both of us enter the arrangement with the gambler's abandon, which is genuine commitment, and because we *do* have such a stake, we are far more likely to be able to get over the rough places together.

The birth of a child is likewise an amazing gamble. Two persons become responsible for the appearance of a third, one who has never been in existence before. There is no way of determining even the sex of the child, to say nothing of his temperament and destiny. There is always a chance of physical deformity; there is always a chance of mental abnormality; there is always the chance that the child may become an evil person, shaming his own parents by his subsequent deeds. He may, in spite of tender goodness, be destined to undergo terrible pain and may meet death before the promise of his life is fulfilled.

In the face of all such contingencies it may seem surprising that men and women become parents at all, since, thanks to modern inventions, parenthood is not really a necessity. Yet millions are born annually, not merely among backward people who presumably are not wholly aware of the dangers, but also among the most thoughtful and advanced who understand reasonably well what the dangers are, including the dangers of war. This tendency to go boldly forward, in spite of dangers, when we cannot possibly see our way to the end, far from being an illogical weakness, is one of the more glorious aspects of human life. If men and women were always to refuse to act until all the evidence were in, nearly all that is finest in human experience would be sacrificed.

What is glorious is not the "Will to Believe" in the sense that we allow our wishes or desires to affect our judgment, in the face of stubborn facts, but rather the will to act in the light of commitment. We must realize, with genuine intellectual humility, that we can be wrong, yet determined to prove our position in the only way in which it can be proved. We do this, as was suggested in Chapter VI, whenever we choose and follow a vocation. We are really making a wager on our own powers and upon the way in which we can render the most significant contribution. If we were to wait for all the evidence to come in, we should wait until we were seventy years old or older, but then it would be too late. We must decide, and then having decided, our wager on our work is the only way in which the rightness of our decision can be proved. The investment of time and energy is so great that it constitutes a genuine gambling act.

There is something fundamentally immoderate about the plan of life outlined in this chapter, but this we must accept unapologetically. The rewards of moderation are actually extremely modest rewards, however much it may be advised by the prudent of all ages. The dangers of moderation are, paradoxically, greater than are the dangers of excess, because the wholly moderate person is so likely to become balanced on dead center, and consequently to accomplish nothing. The wholly balanced judgment is the ineffective judgment. This seems to have been the major point of that wise man, the late

Professor Whitehead, when he wrote, "A certain excessiveness is an indispensable ingredient of greatness."

It is well known that Aristotle included, in his famous ethical treatise, the idea that the good life is a mean between two extremes. Thus true courage is neither the rashness of the man who throws his life away nor the cowardice of the person who protects his own interest completely, but rather a third position midway between these. Aristotle's point is that the good man is the moderate man. But, of all that Aristotle wrote on ethical questions, this is the part that has received the least corroboration in subsequent thought. Great as many of his insights undoubtedly were, there were points on which Aristotle was wrong and this is one of them. In any case, moderation is not a Christian virtue since the basic Christian teaching is far closer to rashness than to prudence. The word "moderation" is not in the Bible.[2]

The glorious ideal of immoderation is seen at its best in generosity. This is not only or chiefly generosity in money, important as that is, but generosity in our judgments of one another. We are familiar with the man who is stingy with his praise, being constantly fearful that he may overstate himself or make some other person temporarily conceited. The worst effect of this verbal stinginess lies in the drying up effect it has on the stingy man himself. The man who sees that moderation is largely a vice will run the risk of erring on the side of being overgenerous, and he will run it gladly. This he ought to do, not because, prudentially, the bread thus cast upon the waters will return to him, but because, in the light of man's nature,

[2] It appears to be in Phil. 4:5, but only because of a mistranslation in the King James Version. The word is really "forbearance."

appreciation is itself a good. It is, other things being equal, a better world in which men are profligate in their praise than one in which they are miserly.

Illustrations of the value of excessiveness abound in biographical literature. Such a one appears in the fierce struggle between Woodrow Wilson and his opponents in guiding the destinies of Princeton University, under Wilson's presidency of that institution. Ray Stannard Baker, Wilson's biographer, tells how Dean West, Wilson's bitter opponent, had an extreme or immoderate desire for academic beauty and how this, unbalanced as it was, did bring results in the development of the university. "So many of the good things of the world," concludes Baker, "come out of an excess of qualities, an excess of devotion or enthusiasm, an excess of faith, that sometime limits or destroys the possessor of it." Wilson's own adherence to the ideal of the League of Nations might be cited as one justification of the same conclusion on the part of his biographer.

It is not the poise of perfect balance that moves mankind forward on his zigzag path, but the glorious immoderation of those who see something so clearly that they are willing to live and die for it. Such abandon seems tumultuous, but it actually produces a species of inner peace, for it helps to overcome crippling anxiety. The only way in which a man can move forward in what we call walking is by always being slightly out of balance, since the perfectly balanced man stands still. History moves forward as the balance is recurrently broken and restored.

If these well-tested insights are true, we have a glimpse of the mood in which the ordinary lives of ordinary people should be lived. There is no inconsistency about being tender toward

others and yet bold in the living of our lives. Each of us has one
life to live, and much as we belong together there are some
ways in which each is fundamentally alone. Each must decide
ultimately how he will spend the one life he has, since it is only
by being spent that any life has true value. In all the great
things the best man is an unashamed spendthrift.

Each of us is bound to die, and every rational person is highly
conscious that his life is short, but there need be no tragedy in
this. It is surely not so bad to die, providing one has really
lived *before* he dies. Life need not be long to be good, for indeed it cannot be long. The tragedy is not that all die, but that
so many fail really to live. The chief way in which men miss
much of the possible richness of living is by playing the game
safely, seeking always to avoid all risk. The problem of every
man is how he will sell his life and, if he is wise, he will sell it
high. But this is not possible except in terms of a wager. The
best life is one in which, committed to some cause which has
won our full loyalty, we give ourselves and all our energies to
it in uncalculating and unmercenary devotion. Such lives have
actually been lived, and, when we see them, we know that
they are good.

The philosophy enunciated in this chapter has a bearing on
our lives as individuals, but the bearing on our group life may
be even more important and striking. The tradition of Western
man which we have reason to honor, in spite of its injustices
and failures, has been a tradition of courage. Ours, for better
or for worse, is a heritage of brave men and women in tiny
ships, setting out, with their little ones, for relatively unknown
and dangerous territories. It is not mere bombast to say that

the cowards never started and that the weaklings died on the way.

In spite of the absurdity of the conventional Western stories, so adaptable to the technique of the motion picture, the underlying conception of the glory of the westward trek is sound. Our fathers and mothers *did* move into the new land in covered wagons; they *did* push back the frontier, and theirs was an enterprise in which the timid did not succeed. They did terrible things and they stole the land from the original owners, but, for the most part, they were not cowards. Now that the physical frontier is gone, we must, if we are to honor our heritage and avoid its palpable mistakes, enter new tasks in which the pioneering spirit is still needed and where it can find full scope.

Our danger is that we may now appear to the world, and even to ourselves, as the *settled* people, trying to hold on to what we and our fathers have accumulated, whether of money, of power, of prestige or of culture. But since a society which has ceased to advance is already in full decay, we must resist, at all costs, being cast in this unexciting role. The civilized man makes the *dwelling*, as Saint Exupéry says, but it is likewise true that each generation must somehow *expand* it. We cannot defend ourselves permanently if our major mood is the mood of defense; we must attack, and we must attack in the realm of ideas. The frontier for our time lies where men may create, not new towns, but new imagination about the ways in which man's life may be improved on this planet. We could, given sufficient good will, overcome the dread specter of starvation in all parts of our troubled planet. The major problem here is not the scientific one, since scientific agriculture is so well advanced that the earth can be made to produce sufficient food for all its inhabitants. The bulging and increasingly numerous steel granaries in all of the grain-producing states and provinces of North America provide eloquent witness in this connection. The phenomenal increase of food production which hybrid seed corn has made possible is only one illustration, though perhaps the most revolutionary, of what can be accomplished when men try.

It is well known that the most successful card which the men of the Kremlin have played, during the past thirty years, has been the dream of a revolutionary world order, which has convinced many of the suppressed millions that it holds a hope for altered conditions of living for them. But if we who prize the life of the West are really loyal to the faith which has actuated the best we have, and if we can combine our idea of the infinite value of personality with boldness of imagination in putting it into effect, we can present the perplexed peoples of the earth with a dream far more exciting than that advertised by the Kremlin. Only as we do so, shall we avoid being outmaneuvered, whatever happens in a military way.

What we must sell, and really mean, is a new social vision. It is possible to avoid many diseases which millions now take for granted; it is possible to have a measure of economic security; it is possible to win the battle against hunger; and it is possible to do all this without the use of concentration camps for dissenters. If we enter bold enterprises, such as those envisaged in President Truman's Point Four, we shall find them very expensive, but a continual war of defense, even without official declaration, is even more expensive and there seems to be no escape from such warfare, except as some bold ideological advance catches the imagination of large sections of the world's population.

We must learn to wage peace as boldly as we wage war, and with far more imagination. Since it is obviously intolerable that the present world tension between two balanced parts should go on permanently, we must find some way to end it. If we try to end it by war we may pay a price so fantastic that our very effort becomes self-defeating. Because the Stalinist idea is not likely to change or to fall into quick decay, the only practical alternative is an ideological advance *on our part*. The point is that a modest experiment will have almost no effect. "Make no small plans; they have no power to move men's hearts." Unless our proposals are *bold* they will be ineffective. It is no part of the author's purpose in this particular book to try to give a detailed picture of what a program of world reconstruction should be, but it is a part of his purpose to maintain that enlightened imagination in this field is the most important business that can engage the best minds at this juncture of human history. Most of the disciplined imagination in this field is still waiting to be done. That part of the frontier is still open.

IX

THE RESPONSE TO SUFFERING

Whoever among us has through personal experience learned what pain and anxiety really are . . . belongs no more to himself alone; he is the brother of all who suffer.

—ALBERT SCHWEITZER

No philosophy of life can have anything like completeness without a frank acceptance of the fact that, in spite of our best efforts, life often goes wrong. We do our very best to overcome illness and disease, but these are still with us, and may be, in one form or another, to the end. In every generation there are the terribly handicapped, those with disfigured faces, those with disfigured bodies, those with very little strength or physical endurance. Some have inherited tendencies to mental illness which cause them to be more anxious than others; some struggle hopelessly with incipient insanity; some are embittered all their lives by the realization that they have not had a fair deal. A bold program of world reconstruction could help to eliminate some of the causes of human misery, but it could never eliminate all.

The amount of sheer physical suffering at any moment, even in the human family, is staggering to contemplate, though this is only a tiny fraction of the pain constantly being borne on this planet. Thousands are daily dying of cancer and other thousands are so crippled that they must be carried wherever they go. Not all have suffered equally, but any loving parent can imagine what it is to see his happy little child stricken with infantile paralysis with the expectation that he will never run again. The loss of lives in war is terrible to contemplate, particularly in its wastefulness of what we cannot afford to lose, but the maiming of the bodies and the shattering of the minds of those who survive the conflict may be even worse. Though there is a profound sense in which it is true that all men are created equal, as the Declaration of Independence says, and as we have discussed in Chapter V, in nearly all of the less profound senses they are created strikingly unequal. Men are not equal in talents, in intelligence, in strength, in opportunities. Some seem to have a magic carpet laid in front of them, but millions of others seem to be born to misfortune even in the most favored lands. They begin with frail bodies, and they are doomed to struggle all their lives with grinding poverty. For great numbers of the human race such a possession as a fountain pen or a gold watch is manifestly impossible. And we must never forget, as we discuss the state of the world, while we sip our after-dinner coffee, that many of our fellow men are actually hungry and many more live near the hunger line.

If we are to be honest in our thinking we must never fail to look directly at such facts as these or try to explain them away. Even those philosophies which hold that all pain is illusory must nevertheless deal with the fact that all of us share the illusion and that the illusion is quite as difficult to explain as the reality could ever be. Ours, whatever the explanation, is a world in which there is not only happiness, actual and potential, but also a vast amount of sorrow. Ours is a struggle in which many lives are undoubtedly fortunate, but it is also one in which many fail all the time and the others fail some of the time. The gospel of success has a certain plausibility, for men *can* succeed, at least for a while, but this gospel is always severely restricted in its appeal because only a minority taste success, whereas failure is universal. This may be the reason for the profound appeal of tragedy, which reaches deep places in men's hearts that comedy can never touch. It may seem strange, in view of our apparent interest in happiness, that *Paradise Lost* appeals as *Paradise Regained* never can, but it is true. It is not mere poetic license to say, "Our sweetest songs are those that tell of saddest thought."

In view of the general purpose of this book, it is neither necessary nor wise to include a chapter on the Problem of Evil, but the presentation of the life we prize would be incomplete without an attempt to state the tested wisdom of many generations of thinkers about the way in which men and women ought to live in view of the fact that both they and their fellow men suffer. Our task is not to try to explain how evil arose, but to accept it as a fact and try to discern how we may face it wisely and well. The problem is extremely timely, because, though we have been able to lessen or eliminate some forms of human suffering, our generation has evolved new forms of its own.

What we seek to know is whether those who have given their minds to these matters have found something to say to those who are sorely troubled by the world's pain, inequality and injustice. Ultimately, of course, each person who faces hardship or loss and is thereby tempted to bitterness, must make his own peace and make it alone. There is no medicine for this illness that is effective when externally applied. But this observation does not mean that all words are worthless. There are, indeed, considerations which may help the individual enormously even though the basic struggle is his own. There is a garnered wisdom on the subject of adversity which has been tested by generations of experience more adequately than in almost any other field of thought.

The danger, in expressing this garnered wisdom, is the danger of falling into conventional modes of comfort which sound like pious platitudes with no real substance. This we must avoid at all costs, because the wounded man rightly feels insulted when the fortunate man proffers him cheap and easy advice. No man dares say anything on the problem of suffering unless it is wrung out of his own experience, vicarious or direct, in such a way that not one word is said for mere effect. There is no subject where true wisdom is more precious and likewise no subject where fraudulent wisdom is more transparent. It would be wrong to avoid the subject of how adversity is to be borne, but the author who writes on it is skating on thin ice. Judging by human experience and reflection, and limiting ourselves to that context, there are at least three things of importance that can be said.

In the first place, it is worth while to show that suffering *can* be redemptive. A man who never experienced anything but success would be an unbearable companion, while a certain amount of failure may serve to temper a man. It is good for us to know our size, to realize that we do not always win. A man who always had excellent health, business success, professional advancement, popular approval and ability to win others to himself in close friendship would be superficially happy, but he would be almost sure to miss the possible richness of human experience. He would miss it because his self-confidence would become a kind of self-worship and life would accordingly seem simple. But to see life simply is always to see it falsely, since the deepest truths are the truths of paradox. Only those who have suffered much begin to understand what the secrets of life are and they cannot communicate them except to those who have suffered equally. Part of the secret is that there seems to be a close connection between suffering and love. Love, we agree, is the greatest thing in the world, yet the experience of it, in any full measure, does not come to all, but only to the prepared. And an essential element in the fullest preparation seems to be suffering. Suffering can be especially effective in bringing to men and women a sense of *being loved*.

The problem of evil is not wholly answered by the fact that suffering can be redemptive of human character, but this fact greatly lessens the force of that problem. There are many persons alive today who, having gone through deep personal tragedy and ultimately made their peace with the situation, have a quality in their peace which was not possible before the struggle. When we see this we are still troubled by the fact that some people seem to have far too much sorrow while others seem not to have their share, but we cannot honestly say that it would be a better world if there were no sorrow in it. It looks as though the goal to which our world is pointing, in the development of character, is not mere happiness, but something deeper. This is one of the best indications we have of the ultimate nature of the universe. Ours is a universe of turmoil and even our solar system, it is widely believed by experts, began with a major disturbance. Starting in the tumult of great tides, the history of our own small planet has itself been tumultuous. There has been the fierceness of cold and heat, the harsh struggle for survival, the rise and fall of species. But it all seems to be pointing somewhere, in the direction of more life, more mind, more spirit in the sense of the self-conscious appreciation of what ought to be. Could it have come without the tumult, the pain and the endless struggle? That we do not know, but we *can* see that the emergence of character is an end so good that it justifies all the struggle, no matter how many millions of years it has been in the making. A truly good person is so precious, and such a wonderful product in our universe of space and stars, that any amount of pain and turmoil are justified by the ultimate emergence of this product. If sorrow and defeat and tragedy are the necessary price for the tender courage which we sometimes see on some faces, we may be sure that the price is not too high.

The truth of this conclusion becomes credible when we contrast such faces, tried as it were by fire, with those of the superficial, pleasure-seeking persons that we so often see in contemporary Western life. It is part of the comforting creed of millions that they can avoid all suffering, satisfy their appetites and live in a continual round of self-indulgence. Though few can succeed long at this enterprise, some succeed for a while, but they have their reward! They seek the superficial and they get it, but they miss all that makes life transcendently lovely.

A second consideration is that some of the greatest significance in human life is revealed, not merely in the bearing of pain, but in the concerted effort to overcome it in others. Rich as those lives are which have endured suffering, they seldom fall into the blasphemy of saying that suffering is a good and therefore something to be encouraged or even overlooked. It is an *evil*, but the truth is that ours is a world in which evil may be transcended by being faced and conquered. The paradox is that, frequently, the people who are most resolute in seeking to overcome the world's suffering are the very ones who have been deepened by the struggle with it.

Dr. Albert Schweitzer has fastened upon something of universal appeal in his attempt to form the Fellowship of those who bear the Mark of Pain. Deeply moved by the fact that there are millions in the world without the benefit of anaesthetics and that the torture of suffering which they frequently endure is quite as great as that of others who do have the advantage of the use of drugs, Dr. Schweitzer calls on all who have themselves been in pain to join together to seek to eliminate it, especially among their less fortunate brethren. It is a highly sobering truth that much of human misery is of man's making and that, accordingly, much can be eliminated by human effort. So far as the Western World is concerned, some diseases have already been overcome or made extremely rare and we may be sure that others will soon be in the same category. We have only to wander in any ancient cemetery, observing the many graves of little children, to realize what a change has come in infant mortality. With modern methods of public health this amazing boon can be given to backward peoples, though with incalculable effects on shifts in population. It is reasonable to expect that the conquest of cancer may be successful in the lifetime of many now living.

In the loyal service of the Fellowship of those who bear the Mark of Pain, many, throughout the centuries, have found wholeness of life. The phrase is Dr. Schweitzer's, but the idea is very old, and its value has been continually proved in the history of our race. Human character seems to reach something of its possible fullness when the attention is centered on the pain and suffering and tragedy of others. Men are embittered by contemplating, very much, their own misfortunes, for they soon become sorry for themselves and deeply self-centered in consequence. They are, however, lifted and ennobled when they concentrate their attention on the effort to remove the pain of other men and women.

Here again is the flair for objectivity which has been mentioned several times in our previous discussion and which, in so many different ways, provides a key to the good life. The stronger a man's character becomes, the less attention he pays to his own ills and the more tender he becomes in his attention to the ills of others. His life is unified by a focus of attention outside his own consciousness, and this brings both unity and mental health, though these are not the ends sought. Contemplation of the suffering of others, particularly when it eventuates in some active service, may give a person such a keen sense of solidarity with his fellows that he practically loses his sense of separateness. Vicariously, he so feels the pain of others that the ordinary distinctions of mine and thine become practically meaningless.

This sense of solidarity in the experience of suffering, a solidarity which mere pleasure can never produce, has been expressed in remarkably similar ways by different generations of men who have seen deeply into the secrets of human life. As they have reached, independently, identical or nearly identical conclusions they have provided corroboration for the

insights of one another and have demonstrated the same kind
of verification which we seek in scientific method. Thus John
Donne, in a passage made famous, even in our day, because it
has provided the title of a popular novel, used a striking figure
to show that sorrow unites man.

No man is an Iland intire of itselfe; every man is a peece of
the Continent, a part of the maine; if a clod bee washed away
by the Sea, Europe is the lesse, as well as if a Promontorie
were, as well as if a Mannor of thy friends or of thine owne
were; any man's death diminishes me, because I am involved
in Mankinde. And therefore never send to know for whom the
bell tolls. It tolls for thee.

More than a century later John Woolman, the humble New
Jersey tailor and perhaps the most saintly man whom America
has produced, was so moved by the sufferings of his fellows,
particularly those who were slaves, that he felt as though he
were a slave too. A few weeks before he died of smallpox, in
1772, Woolman was traveling in the north of England and had
leisure there to write the following account which is similar
to that of Donne, though it is practically certain that he had
never read Donne's words:

In a time of sickness, a little more than two years and a half
ago, I was so near the gates of death that I forgot my name.
Being then desirous to know who I was, I saw a mass of matter
of a dull gloomy colour between the south and the east, and
was informed that this mass was human beings in as great
misery as they could be and live, and that I was mixed with
them, and that henceforth I might not consider myself a dis-
tinct or separate being. I then heard a soft, melodious voice,
more pure and harmonious than any I had heard with my ears
before; . . . the words were "John Woolman is dead." . . .
Then the mystery was opened and I perceived . . . that the

language "John Woolman is dead," meant no more than the death of my own will.

Again, in the nineteenth century, we find Walt Whitman singing the "Song of Myself" which turned out to be the song of solidarity with struggling humanity. Whitman was greatly different from both Donne and Woolman, but he spoke a language similar to theirs when he said,

> Whoever degrades another degrades me,
> And whatever is done or said returns at last to me.

Years later in our own century, Eugene V. Debs, having been imprisoned for the sake of what seemed to him a matter of principle, and having secured, while in prison, almost a million votes for President of the United States, joined the fellowship of verification by writing, "As long as there is a man in prison I am not free."

Lofty utterances, such as these four, from four different centuries, represent not something rare and unusual in human life, but something that can dignify the experience of the most humble as well as the highly gifted. There is no more wonderful thing than the effort to reduce the burdens of others by the simple act of sharing them. Here is a response to adversity which could be universal and which, though it does not explain evil, gives men and women a task which glorifies common lives. All men can face the problem of adversity by seeking to reduce or to avoid as much as possible of the pain of their fellow men, regardless of where they live and what ideology they espouse. In the long run, this is what pierces all curtains.

A third factor in a practical philosophy, as far as the problem of harmful suffering is concerned, refers to the apparently unfair distribution of human powers. How can a man keep from bitterness when he knows he is suffering from a terrible handicap? Is it fair to let the crippled race with the strong? Is it fair to expect a man to labor when he is blind? Is it fair to ask a man to speak when his mouth is ill-formed?

There is an ancient answer to this that is still valid, to the effect that we are accountable only for what is given. We are not responsible for the hand that has been dealt us, but we *are* responsible for the way in which we play it. Wisdom comes in distinguishing between what is in our power and what is beyond our power. To complain about what is beyond our power, our original endowment, is to engage in fruitless and vain effort, but there is always something that is *not* fruitless and vain. What is really within our power and therefore worthy of attention is the particular use we make of the powers given us. These we have as a sacred trust, whether they be few or many, and every man's life can be glorified by using well whatever he has.

In our modern world it is a handicap in life's struggle to be born a Negro, but how shall those who have this handicap face it? Certainly not by any fruitless regret at not having been born white. Many have shown the true way of life by accepting frankly this handicap, without in any sense minimizing it, and then showing the world the peculiar worth that may be possible in the career of a person of color. The responsibility of a Negro is not to be a Caucasian, but to demonstrate the best of Negro life, which may have depths of feeling that no white person knows. In a similar way it is a handicap to be blind, yet the way out is not by pining for a vanished sight, but by an exploration of the richness that a blind man's life holds. Perhaps there are some truths revealed to the blind which no man of normal sight may see. Certainly authentic revelations have come to those with frail and broken bodies, which have been hidden from the self-satisfied and healthy persons whom we call normal.

There is truly a law of compensation to the effect that the loss of one power frequently encourages the development of others. The woman long confined to bed with illness may read far more than the person carrying on normal duties can possibly find time to read. The deaf can develop marvelous powers of meditation, released as they are from the chitchat of ordinary conversation. One of the most valued personal counselors on any American college campus is a man who became totally blind at the age of twelve. This man, now at the height of his powers, is admitted to have a place of influence among thousands of students such as none of his teaching and administrative colleagues can have, because he has exploited to the full the advantages of being blind.

Every life, even the most normal one, is limited because we have so many more powers than we can possibly develop concurrently. Since we cannot properly develop all of our powers, we must choose a few and neglect the others. The handicapped person is one for whom the choice is already partly made, but, after this, his position is not as different as we normally suppose it to be.

There is one adversity which we ought to emphasize by separate treatment because it seems to have about it a finality which most other adversities do not have. This is the pain involved in the fact that men and women *die*. There is, indeed, no proposition of which we are more certain than the affirmation that we shall die. For the most part we give this conviction little attention, but it lies, nevertheless, in our subconsciousness. We know, when we allow ourselves to think about it at all, that, even if we have a few more years to live, no person has many. In less than a hundred years nearly all who are now alive will have become memories, so far as earthly life is concerned.

Sobering as the thought of our own death may be, it presents no baffling problem. Of course we shall die, and why not? It is pointless to complain. A world in which people could never die would be far worse than one in which death is the lot of all, because there would be no room for anyone to live. A world without death, with the consequent crowding and the stultification of the living, is really self-contradictory. Furthermore, death is by no means always a tragedy. Thousands each year welcome it, because they find the burden of pain or disease or loneliness intolerable. We know that it is unreasonable to value anything and not, at the same time, willingly pay its necessary price. Part of the glory of life is its delicacy of balance, but if we have a delicate balance, we have a balance that can be disturbed.

The prospect of death may seem frightening and terrible to a child, partly because he sees the future with such inadequate perspective and partly because he does not have the advantage of the philosophical approach which may help those of wider reading and more mature years, but, for the mature person, the fear is greatly diminished or sometimes wholly removed. So far as mature persons are concerned, it is seldom their own death that worries them. Indeed the man who is always concerned with his own end is probably mentally ill. If we are healthy-minded we realize that we are not indispensable and that, if the need should arise, there are hundreds of causes for which we would gladly give up our little lives.

But what does disturb us is the prospect of the loss of those whom we greatly honor and deeply love. Plato gave no indication of concern over his own inevitable end, but he was moved beyond measure by the death of Socrates. It was the unreasonableness of supposing that the mere cessation of bodily functions could wholly obliterate the mind of a man of the character of Socrates, that drove Plato to the inquiry which bore fruit in the *Phaedo*. Not many men are greatly worried over immortality for themselves and few are driven to believe in it as a means of self-encouragement, but millions find it impossible to believe that the world, which has in it so many hints of meaning and rationality, could also include the wanton waste of destroying, at death, those characters which appear, to date, to be the chief justification of the cosmic process.

There is no great need of a philosophy to bolster a man's mind in the face of his own inevitable demise, but he does need a philosophy to bolster him when he loses what is nearest and dearest. The experience is hardest to bear when the loved person is in the fullness of his powers or in the bloom of youth. There is nothing tragic or even sad about the death of an old person, whose work is done and whose remaining days, even if there were a few more, might be burdensome, both to himself and to others. In fact, if we were reasonable, a memorial service at the end of a long and fruitful career, far from being a time of weeping, would be a time of thanksgiving and joy. It might be expected that the friends and neighbors would gather to express gratitude that such a life had been lived and that they had had the privilege of sharing it. The body might well be returned to earth with songs of jubilation.

Most persons in the modern world make the mistake of avoiding any serious consideration of death in the time when it is possible to consider it dispassionately. The consequence is that the average family has no plans made about even such details as funeral service and place of burial, but decisions on these matters must be made eventually and often suddenly. When there has been no preparatory thought the forced decisions are painful, and what might have been a means of satisfaction becomes a burden. It is part of the wisdom of life to prepare to face death, particularly of those under our care, not with any morbid preoccupation with sorrow, but with the calm realization that the best path for men lies in doing well what is inevitable. They bear tragedy best who have, in advance, the best inner resources. It is a deepening experience for a person to ask himself, in the midst of his happiness which seems so secure, how he could go forward if he should lose suddenly that which he prizes most.

Though we may truly say that death is no serious problem, so far as the individual alone is concerned, and likewise that it is no problem in the case of the aged, including one's own parents in advanced years, it is a terrible problem when we face the loss of those of younger years. The problem is terrible because, in addition to the inevitable sense of loneliness, there is also the sense of waste. Here was a life which the world needed, which might have been productive over many years, yet, for no apparent good end, it is cut off in a twinkling. The attractive young son, an only child, leaves home gaily and, before an hour is elapsed, he is dying in the wreck of an automobile accident. Another boy, twenty years of age, is drafted, sent to the battle front and in a few days is dead of bullet wounds. A beautiful girl, in the first bloom of young womanhood, is stricken with a disease and dies as her fond parents watch helplessly. A young husband sees his wife of one year breathe her last as her baby is born. What shall we say to those who grieve when the loss is genuinely tragic? The easy words of conventional comfort seem like an affront.

Anyone who has ever been in a position of a counselor knows that illustrations of genuine personal tragedy, such as those mentioned above, far from being imaginary, are part of the stuff of ordinary life. The professor is in his study, preparing for a lecture, when a boy enters and says, "You know about the plane that was lost yesterday? Well, the pilot was my father." What does the professor say then?

We may be utterly sure that the sense of hurt will never be wholly removed from some lives. When a man has been bitter for twenty years over the death of a beloved child, no easy answer is likely to change him now. But there may be some considerations that *help*, and it is to these that we should turn our attention. Each reader may ask, "What would help me if I were to lose my nearest and dearest?" Is there any garnered wisdom? Surely there must be, for men and women have faced such loss from the beginning of human history and the pain of our early ancestors in this situation must have been quite as great as our own. Some of them must have found a way of life even in the valley of shadow.

There are at least three considerations which, even in a purely human context, may help us. There are others besides these, but they are no part of this chapter since they depend upon faith and will therefore be reserved for the final chapter.

The first consideration is that, whatever we lose, we can be grateful for what we have already had. No tragedy of the present can eliminate or alter the past. If I have known and loved my child for twenty years, I have in that experience something of ineffable value and something of which I know I am unworthy. I hoped it would continue, but duration is not essential to value. One life of twenty years may be far more significant than other lives of a hundred. The son of John Gunther, of whom the journalist has written so tenderly, did not live to be an old man, but that fact seems actually almost irrelevant. It is quality of living that counts and a life may be viewed as, in one sense, a finished product, even if it seems to be cut off in mid-course.

Though all quickly realize that the completion of an old person's life may be hailed with joy, rather than tears, it seems, at first, fantastic to suggest the same for the young. Yet this could be reasonable. Is it not better for this beautiful girl to have lived fifteen years than never to have lived at all? She might not have been, but she *was*. If this life, in spite of its sudden end, was an undeserved blessing, we ought to say so. We have, by this young life, been given some new hint of the richness of experience which our mysterious world holds, and we can be gloriously grateful for it.

A second consideration is that we can be consciously loyal to the ones whom we have lost and thus continue their lives vicariously in our own work. We can transmute our sorrow, which, left to itself, becomes self-pity or even self-indulgence, into some concrete task for the betterment of the rest of mankind. Since our boy is not able to carry on the work that he might have done, we who remain must, in loyalty to him, carry it on in his stead. Thus a lady in Philadelphia, losing her only son as a medical student, used her spacious home for many years to help other boys to complete their medical training. It is wholly possible that, by this means, the son's death actually contributed more to medicine than his continued life could have done.

One of the most appealing stories of the transmutation of sorrow into objective work is that of John Bright, as he faced, broken-hearted, the death of his young wife. Richard Cobden came to Bright and suggested that the noblest way in which he could face his personal sorrow was to throw his energies into a crusade for the repeal of the corn laws of England and the consequent improvement of the life of the poor. Bright accepted the challenge, and gave himself single-mindedly to the new task, with well-known results. He did not love his dead wife the less, but he learned to make his private sorrow a source of public good and, in so doing, honored his wife far more than if he had spent his days sorrowing alone and pining for what could never again be.

The late Rufus Jones had only one son, Lowell, who died at the age of eleven, but the boy continued, for forty-five more years, to be a dominant influence in the great man's life. The Jones' study at Haverford included many photographs of the learned and famous, but the central place, over the mantle, was always occupied by the portrait of this boy. Rufus Jones felt that he had to live for both himself and his boy, and in this he succeeded, to a remarkable degree. Writing more than forty years after the occasion of his sorrow, Rufus Jones told of the boy as follows: "I overheard him once talking with a group of playmates, when each one was telling what he wanted to be when grown up, and Lowell said when his turn came, 'I want to grow up and be a man like my daddy.' Few things in my life have ever touched me as those words did, or have given me a greater impulse to dedication. What kind of a man was I going to be, if I was to be the pattern for my boy!"

Who can say, when he contemplates a story like this, that the death of the eleven-year-old son was really a tragic waste? Are we so sure that it would have been better, in the long run, had the son lived out the normal lifetime? In any case it is clear that the stricken father, by fighting his inner battle and coming out victorious, was always, after that, both stronger and more tender than he could have been apart from this moving experience. The loss may still be terrible, but ours is a world in which it can be transmuted into human gain.

A third consideration is the fact that our own personal sorrow can be greatly lessened, or at least glorified, by being shared. At first, when our friends face some heavy blow, the very best that we can do is to assure them of our continued affection and to try to share the suffering. The expression of continued affection has the immense advantage that it can always be offered without the fear of seeming to engage in conventionalized comfort. When a man has lost what he prizes most, he does not wish to hear some pious remark minimizing his loss, but he does wish to hear from those who agree with him that the loss is great and who know what they are talking about. What really helps is to have a friend say, "I understand in part, for I loved her too."

Sometimes, when a person has lost his life partner or his

child, we fear to mention the subject, thinking that we thereby reopen the wound. Actually, however, we often harm the bereaved by our refusal to mention the subject. In most instances, the wounded person craves the chance to talk about his loss, providing it can be faced frankly with someone who also cares. A man who has lost his wife loves to hear ever more about her from those who knew her when she was young, from those who admired her, from those who profited by her generosity. Each such report makes him know that his loss is real rather than fanciful. Even after the long years of separation this is still true and one of the kindest of acts is to become a willing listener while the bereaved tells of his beloved without the fear of boring. Our adage to the effect that time heals all wounds is not wholly true. The best of healing medicine is not time, but *sharing*.

What we have now said is the best that we can say within the limitations which we have set ourselves in the main portion of this book. What we have said we can say honestly, without any suggestion of cant, and it *is* some help. But honesty compels us to say also that it is inadequate. Without something more, life is bearable and may, at times, be beautiful, but the undertones are inevitably sad. There are many in our modern world who, in intellectual honesty, cannot go further, and the accumulated human wisdom, such as that which this chapter seeks to present, will be their only comfort in life's darkest moments. What is perhaps most revealing is how little, upon this basis alone, there is to say.

X

A BASIC FAITH

And yet show I unto you a more excellent way.
—ST. PAUL

The moral structure of the life of the West, to the depiction of which the preceding chapters are devoted, does not stand alone, without support. In addition to this moral structure, and usually assumed by it, is a basic faith which cuts across many lines, both national and sectarian, by which we are often separated. In great measure this basic faith is the real inspiration of the life we prize and this is true even when the source of the inspiration is unrecognized. To understand or to describe the life we prize without reference to our religion is an impossible task, yet any reference to it is fraught with great difficulty.

The difficulty we face is a double one in that, on the one hand, millions in our culture believe they have outgrown and discarded the faith which originally gave us most of our moral structure, while, on the other hand, those who continue to hold, with deep conviction, religious beliefs, seem to be tragically divided among themselves. Is not any general statement of faith likely to be rejected by one group on the ground that it is *false* and by all sections of the other group on the ground that it is *inadequate*?

The careful reader may have been surprised to find in this

volume so far, not only the general avoidance of the professional language of philosophy, but also of the professional language of religion. This avoidance has been deliberate, because such language would alienate many of the very readers whose good opinion I value and whose minds I am eager to reach. I have tried to start with my neighbor where he is willing to start and to walk with him as far as he is willing to go. There are millions in our modern world who would never, knowingly, read a religious book, but who, at the same time, are deeply concerned about man's plight and are willing to engage in any promising effort to improve his sad condition. Some such readers might actually be more sympathetic with the thoughts already expressed than their apparently more religious neighbors would be. Accordingly the book, up to this point, has been written in a consciously secular mood, but it cannot be ended that way, because to do so would be to leave the structure hanging in mid-air. The final chapter, in a different mood, is added, not as an appendix, but as a logical necessity if the rest is to stand.

Some of the convictions which undergird our present ideal of life in what we call the free world came from ancient Greece, but, to a far greater degree, they came from Palestine. It is from the Hebrew heritage, with its conviction that all are made in God's image, that we get something which is strong enough to make the democratic ideal credible. As this faith flowered in the life and message of Christ, the notion that each human being is intrinsically valuable was given added support by reference to God's love for each one, no matter how worthless in the eyes of his fellow men. If every man, regardless of race or knowledge or fortune, is an object of God's care, and one for whom Christ died, then the idea of respect for persons begins to make sense and democracy, or something like it, is the only tenable pattern of life for men. The revolutionary ideas of equality and dignity, and consequent due process, come not of themselves, but from such sources. They do not stand alone as interesting inventions, but are corollaries of an experience which millions have found reason to believe is a genuine revelation.

The faith which has existed in the life of the West, not only as the basis of ethical conduct, but also as the mother of the arts, the encourager of science and the founder of schools, is now in partial decay and is widely ignored as irrelevant. On both sides of the World Civil War this faith is substantially rejected, but rejected in different ways. In Russia the situation is that, among the intellectuals, the rejection of religious faith has been thorough and complete, though it may be argued that they have substituted another religion of their own making. The regime no longer finds it necessary to fight the Church, because the new system has collected all the young people under its banner, and there is no danger now involved in being tolerant of the few old people who keep up what the leaders consider an outworn and discredited system. With no youth, the days of the Church are obviously numbered, barring some radical change in the course of events.

On our side of the iron curtain we have, for the most part, a different approach in that we have less outright or conscious atheism. Indeed, it is unpopular, in our present society, to be an atheist. The popular position is to believe that God exists, in some remote and irrelevant manner, but to consider that such a belief involves no special duties or responsibilities. It is common to claim that there is no need of the Church, because individual religion is allegedly sufficient. This combines easily with the supposed axioms that tolerance is the greatest of the virtues and that one religion is as good as another. Since, according to this position, no religious position can be false, those who hold this position never engage in rigorous thought on such matters. There is a vague idea that religious thinking has somehow ceased to be intellectually respectable, but few could say why or how.

Though there is a vast amount of practical irreligion on both sides of the World Civil War, the irreligion of the West is less dogmatic than that of the dialectical materialists and leads more easily to misgivings about its own sufficiency. In a society, admittedly imperfect, in which we nevertheless have constant reminders of our moral tradition, there are always bound to be thoughtful persons who consider seriously the conditions which gave rise to this heritage in its beginnings and who become skeptical of the assumption that the precious flowers can be maintained permanently in separation from the roots to which they were originally attached and by which they were nourished.

It is one of the signs of hope in our troubled time that an increasing number of modern men and women in the West are now restive under the pagan orthodoxy of their generation, especially when they consider seriously the course of world events. Realizing that our conventional paganism has not been wholly successful, they are skeptical of the ability of men to maintain themselves in this slippery middle ground between Stalinism, on the one hand, and unapologetic faith in the Living God, on the other. The words which follow are addressed not

merely to devout believers who may welcome a brief statement, but also to sincere seekers, in the hope that they may
find here the outlines of a faith which, on the one hand, gives
something deeper and firmer to live by than a mere ethical
system can provide, while, on the other hand, it does not outrage either critical intelligence or the love of freedom. Above
all, such a faith is not a psychological device for making
people lose their anxieties. We must resist, all along the line,
the temptation to make a mere means out of what ought to be
an end. We seek a faith which is more than utilitarian. Such a
faith, far from being inconsistent with the ethical ideal presented in the preceding chapters, and equally far from being
an alternative to it, is that without which the ethical ideal is
incomplete. It grounds the ideal in the real.

There are many who suppose that a faith which transcends
the confines of particular denominations is necessarily vague
and minimal. This supposition we utterly reject. The statement which follows is an effort to formulate a faith which,
while it grinds no denominational ax, and while it renounces
the claims of ecclesiastical exclusiveness, is nevertheless definite,
precise and full of meaning. The deep conviction is that the
things that unite us are far more significant, in most cases, than
are the things which separate us, and that those who reject
authoritarian systems, in religion as in politics, may nevertheless have a faith that is positive and clear.

Some sensitive readers must have felt that the preceding
chapters left a strange sense of incompleteness. What has been
said, for instance, about the response to suffering is true, as
far as it goes, but it would be wonderful if we could go further.

We said all that we could truthfully say within the limits of the discussion, on the facing of the death of our loved ones, but at best this is a pathetic ending. The argument about the necessity of loyalty to a cause is sound, both psychologically and ethically, but what cause shall it be? If there is a real solution of the problem raised by the sense of guilt, what is it? The presentation of the life we prize turns out to be like a piece of music which ends without a conclusion, and the very incompleteness haunts us. What we require is a faith which we have reason to think is true and which, *if true*, provides the completion which is otherwise lacking.

Not all readers will be willing to go further, and to those who feel that they cannot, we must hasten to say that a man who has no practical belief in God may nevertheless be a good man. Sometimes it is the very goodness of a man which makes him an unbeliever; he is so superlatively honest, so eager not to accept anything without adequate evidence, so sensitive to the danger of believing what is comforting merely *because* it is comforting, that he rejects the very conception which makes reasonable his intense effort to be honest. Such a man we can only honor, and trust that he will go on loyally following the evidence wherever it leads. It might, eventually, lead him to the sober conviction that his very concern for the truth cannot be explained if it is an alien development, appearing alone in a world completely insensitive to such experience, but that it makes sense if moral concern lies at the heart of all things. He may learn the paradox that his brave unbelief, seen in its full implications, may be one of the chief grounds of the very belief which it rejects. In any case, the world is likely to profit far more by the honest unbeliever than by the wishful believer, who believes because his faith is comforting and has never been seriously tested.

It is my deepest faith that men and women, in their fierce and faltering struggle to find the right way, are *not alone*. It is conceivable, of course, that the only point in the entire universe which has been marked by loyalty and courage and self-denial, for the sake of the right, is our little earth, but I do not believe it. It may be that there is no response to our prayers and none to hear them. It may be that all the remainder of reality, beyond the surface of our planet in the last few thousand years, has been a scene which might be studied by physics, but not one in which ethics has any meaning. It may be that, when our solar system is such that the planet earth is no longer a scene of human habitation, the last concern for goodness will be gone from the universe and the world as a whole will go its way, with no consciousness anywhere of what has thereby been lost.

All this, I say, is conceivable, and if I were to learn, by some infallible means, that it is true, I believe I should try to go on living out my little day as best I might. I think I should still try to be honest and to keep my promises and to be ashamed when I failed, even if such interests were known to be confined to the race of men and even if there were none else who cared. But I trust, at the same time, that I should be wise enough to know that such news would indeed be sad news. A great deal of the lift and joy would necessarily go out of human life. If we were alone in our efforts there would be a constant sense of pathos, because these efforts are truly feeble. We turn frequently against the best that we know and our characters are often weak. Furthermore, we should be well aware that our efforts were, at best, only temporary, since nothing would survive the inevitable decay. If moral insight is an accident in the universe it will not abide.

It is in the light of such possible news that the alternative news is so exciting. Some men believe in God and some do not, but every intelligent person can see that, if God really is and, if we can know it, that is wonderful news indeed! It means that we are not alone; that there is power beyond ourselves waiting to back us up; that the earth's decay is not the end of the story; that the running down of the universe is not final. It means that what is highest in value is deepest in nature, that the things which matter most are not at the mercy of those that matter least. Some men, because the evidence does not convince them, give up such a faith, but insofar as they are intelligent, they are saddened by their decision. A world in which men could know that God is *not*, might have some good qualities, but it would be strikingly short on *joy*.

I have many reasons for believing that man is not alone in his efforts to find the way, the most elementary of which is that ours seems, in so many respects, a reasonable universe. Ours seems to be a world of cause and effect, a fact which receives continually more verification from the advancing success of natural science, but it is essential to the notion of order that there is nothing in the effect that was not already in the cause. Streams do not rise higher than their sources, or as the Greek philosophers put it, we never get something from nothing. I believe they were right. But ours is a world which, in the one part we know best, has actually produced *life* and *mind* and *spirit*. Our world has produced not only those entities which can be studied in physics; it has produced the *physicist*, too. Most remarkable of all it has produced physicists, who, because of considerations which have nothing to do with physics, have banded themselves together for a moral crusade.

How is all this to be explained? If our world is one of order, as we all really believe, then our world must have been, long before mind appeared, the kind of world in which mind was implicit. The more we stress the nonaccidental nature of natural law, the more we are driven to the conviction that the very atoms must have been so arranged in the beginning as to be pointing already to a world marked by the emergence of sages and heroes and saints, as well as millions of common people trying, with much failure and some success, to do what they *ought*.

The notion of a world of atoms already being pointed in the direction of the development of life, mind and spirit is a highly mysterious one, but if God really is and if this is God's world, everything falls into place. Then it is no longer surprising that, in science, we advance to the place where, by rational calculation, we can sometimes predict results. This kinship between reason and nature is what we should expect if the material universe is the creation of the Divine Mind and orderly, *for that reason*. The scientist, far from creating laws, is *discovering* them, which is another way of saying that he is thinking God's thoughts after Him and even his scientific refusal to believe without adequate evidence is an act of reverence.

The first and elementary reason for faith in God, then, is the negative one that the notion of something from nothing is absurd. Belief may have its difficulties, as it does, but they are as nothing compared to the intellecual difficulties of unbelief.

To believe that the long development in the direction of moral sensitivity, with all the small intermediate steps finally making the cumulative event possible, is the result of chance, in the precise sense of that which is wholly devoid of purpose, is to stretch credulity too far. The beginning of belief in God, for many a thoughtful man, is the recognition that the only alternative we can imagine involves too great a miracle, the miracle of cumulative advance by continued accident.

Though this elementary beginning is sound, it is only a beginning, and there is much more to follow. As we go further in faith we soon realize that the strongest reasons for belief are not those of speculation, but those of experience. Man may begin with a recognition of causal necessity and proceed to a distant reverence, but he ends with a more personal link. We join in the vast and cumulative fellowship of verification when we begin to hold converse with God, speak with Him, and open our lives to His Guiding Hand, desiring to be led according to His will for us. Then God is no longer a factor in an argument, but the Companion of our days, who supports us along the way. He becomes our Sustainer and Friend on life's brightest as well as life's darkest moments and we believe in the end, not because we have *inferred* Him, but because we have *known* Him.

It is probably futile to speak of this to those of our generation who have had no hint, in their own experience, of what the Divine Companionship may be. They are likely to start arguments which make them feel wise, arguments about "subjectivity" and "psychological explanation" and "projection" and "conditioning" and "wishful thinking," as though these had not occurred, as possible difficulties, to those who claim that the knowledge of God is both intimate and trustworthy. But the truth is that there are countless persons who have faced all these dangers and difficulties with intellectual honesty and have come out unshaken in their testimony. Many of them give the strongest evidence of all by the quality of their changed lives. The most objective evidence for the truth of faith in God is in the lives of men and women throughout the centuries, who, in humility of heart, have claimed to know Him and who have proved their claim by the difference which their experience has made.

In some ways the character of God is more important, so far as the average seeker is concerned, than is the mere existence of God. Millions admit some kind of shadowy existence, no doubt impressed by the causal argument, but stop there. Numbers of these make a great point in our day in resisting the conception of God as personal. In every case, apparently, this comes as part of the effort to be mature, to avoid the superstitions of childhood, whether of the race or of the individual. Those so motivated often say that they are driven to think of God in some impersonal way, as a great force, but that any personal relationship is to them unthinkable.

Because there is no doubt about the high motives of those who exhibit this tendency to transcend childish notions it is full of hope, and can easily be guided into fruitful channels. It is right that we should be on our guard against superstitions, quick to reject illogical conclusions. But there is nothing illogical or superstitious about belief in God as deeply personal. The personal, of course, has nothing to do with what is merely bodily. To say that God is personal is not to suggest that God *has* a body or that He has any similarity to human form. To be personal is to be not only conscious, but self-conscious, to appreciate value, to entertain purposes, to be aware of ends, to be responsive to the needs and aspirations of other persons. *Now the central point is that, if God is not personal, in such a sense, then God is not the ultimate explanation of that which most requires explanation.* What baffles the materialist is the emergence of personal character in a world of chemical reactions. Only one who is supremely personal, as God is, can be the Ground for the emergence of even the finite personality which we see in our fellows and know intimately in ourselves. If God is only an impersonal force, then the stream *has* risen higher than its source, for we can at least be certain that personality appears in *us*. The growth of personality in a world which is impersonal at its heart, places us right back in our old quandary. The universe must be even more baffling and mysterious than we have ever supposed it could be if the *creature* can exhibit traits of higher level than can the *Creator*. But this is what is involved if we are personal and God is not.

The people who have tried to hold to belief in God, while rejecting the personal aspect of the Divine, have sincerely tried to make an advance over a primitive view, but they have, unfortunately, moved in the wrong direction. Just as life is manifestly superior to matter and as consciousness is superior to mere biological phenomena, the appreciation of personal value is superior to mere awareness of external environment. The line of advance is not *away* from the personal, but toward it and possibly through it. Many who resist the notion of God as personal are, no doubt, trying to avoid what seems at first like a limitation to our size and experience, and this effort is wholesome, but personality is not a limiting conception. Personality is the means of emancipation and enlargement. There is a sense, said Pascal, in which the world includes me, but there is a deeper sense in which I include the world, i.e., in my *comprehension*. It may be that we are only partly personal and that someday we may be far more fully so. But to be more personal is not to be *im*personal. Perhaps God is suprapersonal; He may be completely what we are only in part.

In any case we cannot doubt that much of the faith which we have reason to honor has been a faith based on personal intercourse between men and the Divine Companion. If we can know and love God, it is very strange indeed if God cannot also know and love us. Why should the Creator of the world suffer under a handicap greater than our own? The experience of countless humble men and women is that of a relationship which is not impersonal, and not even in the third person, as when we speak of "Him," but in the second person. It is an experience of "I-thou." Most prayer is couched in the second person and even Jesus began, "I thank *Thee*, O Father." Either God's relation to men is this deeply personal one or all who have reported this experience have been deluded. Only the very bold or the very callow will undertake to maintain that position.

Prayer, which means the knowledge of God by firsthand *acquaintance* rather than by mere *description*, is a turning away from self to the Divine Companion. The purpose of prayer is not to change God's intention, which is already perfectly loving, but rather, by some mysterious process, which in our finiteness we cannot understand, to open channels of grace and power which otherwise are closed. If you can turn to God, at any time of day or night, as naturally and unpretentiously as a child turning to his mother, you have found the secret of the saints.

If God is, indeed, truly personal, as so much of experience indicates, we should expect that His most vivid revelation would necessarily be a personal one. The complete way in which He could be shown to us would not be in the majesty of mountains or in the wonder of the stars or even in the intricacy of a cell, but only in a personal life, sharing, as do our little lives, in both affection and temptation, yet perfect where we are imperfect. The good news is that this has occurred! All other historical persons can be approached or forgotten at will, but there lived One whom men cannot leave alone. He revealed the truth of God and man, not merely by what he taught, but far more by what he did, and above all, by what he *was*.

It is a hopeful fact that, when a truly God-inspired man lives, anywhere, there seems to be general recognition of that tremendous fact. There have been, in many different traditions, great personalities, universally respected, and for these we are grateful. Many have made a divine witness and thereby a genuine revelation. Each of those who has won universal respect, from Buddha and Confucius and Moses to Gandhi and Schweitzer in our own day, has helped us to understand what God is. But there is One who, through centuries and in all cultures, has revealed God supremely. In the person of Christ God is made understandable to man. Much as we admire the great teachers, when we approach reverently the life and death of Jesus the knowledge slowly dawns upon us that here we are in the presence of something radically different. The great teachers have explored the world and their own hearts and, as a consequence, have given flashes of almost incredible genius, but with Jesus, however we may resist the conviction, we find something other than genius. He comes, not as a Seeker, but rather as a Revealer who tells what he knows, not what he has deduced. What others do partially he does completely. Imperfect as was the understanding of his reporters, and much as they were bound by the limitations of the thought forms of their day, nevertheless the gospels preserve enough of the stupendous truth to leave us humble in his presence. Much must have been lost, but much remains and what remains is sufficient to shake any man's complacency, if he will submit his mind humbly to the story. The more often we read the story the more sure we are that men are right in dating all events from the birth of Jesus.

In Christ's short years of public life he seemed to put his chief emphasis on the formation and cultivation of a sacred fellowship, made up of extremely fallible men, but yet a fellowship of such a nature that, rooted in loyalty to him and his kingdom, they could move mountains. At first they were overcome with despair and the boldest of them turned out to be a coward when the going was rough, but when they became assured that their Lord was really a risen and Living Lord, they became bold as lions. Starting with every handicap and with no prestige, political or otherwise, they met the fierce enmity of Rome and the intellectual condescension of Greece, and *won*. Plato's academy came to an end and the Roman Empire was dissolved, but the strangely powerful fellowship of the Living Christ penetrated every avenue of man's life. It has faced bitter persecution from the outside and the bigotry and self-aggrandizement of its own members, but the very gates of hell seem unable to prevail against it.

To this living fellowship of all who love Christ and see in him the very revelation of God I seek to belong. And no man can stop me. I need not ask the permission of any official or undergo any external ceremony, for the reality will suffice. If my fellowship with Christ is real, nothing else is necessary and if it is not real, nothing else is sufficient.

I am deeply aware that mere individual religion, for all its occasional nobility, will not suffice. It is fundamentally parasitic because it receives more than it produces. If all were to follow this lonely road, there would not even be guidebooks for the travelers. I know that I cannot be a Christian in my solitariness; the fellowship is not accidental or auxiliary, but is intrinsic to the very notion of the faith. But no one fellowship, my own or any other, has a monopoly on divine grace or a privileged position. The fellowship, which is the true Church, is not limited to any one kind of building or any one kind of organization, but appears wherever men and women gather together in humble dependence upon God as revealed by Christ. A Christian is one who believes that the Life at the very heart of the universe is like Christ and seeks to live in a fashion loyal to this vision. He is a man whose life is unified by a cause and that cause is the cause of Christ, dynamic in any individual life which yields to it. What we require, as weak and faltering persons, is that we should find, somewhere, a purpose and a direction, a steadiness and a power, adequate to every need of life that really matters. It is the experience of countless men that the cause of Christ actually meets this central need, so that, when a man is in Christ, he is a new creature. It is a change of heart, a deep transformation of our inner being that is required; but the wonder is that it also, in many lives, is actually demonstrated. Far from being a change which begins and ends with a man's own personal character, this change is one which comes in the entire social order.

The enduring fellowship, to which we can now belong, was early effective in ending the practice of infanticide, in working for a higher status for women, and in the criticism of corrupt governments. When Rome was in terrible political and moral decay, Christian men of the stature of Augustine undertook to produce a charter of human life under divine guidance that could lead men out of confusion. In this they were not completely successful, but they did make a difference and the effort has never come completely to an end. The continued effect on the political and social order, while far from perfect or ideal, is still chiefly in the direction of the establishment of human rights, because the salt never wholly loses its savor. If we ever achieve a warless world, the Christian witness will be one of the chief reasons for that achievement.

It is one of the great satisfactions of history that the early followers of Christ began so soon to interpret his life in a universal sense. This was necessary because there has always been a temptation to rule out of Christendom all those who are not conscious followers of the Man of Galilee. If salvation is limited to those who are his conscious followers, what of the millions both before his time and since who have had no chance even to hear his name, much less be touched by the magic of his life? A God who would thus play favorites with His children, condemning some to eternal separation from Himself, while admitting others, and distinguishing between them wholly on a basis of the accidents of history or of geography, over which they had no control, would be more devil than God. Certainly He would not remotely resemble Jesus Christ, who spoke of gathering "from the uttermost parts." But how can we combine logically the universality of God's grace and the conviction that conformity to Christ is *the way*?

The answer of the early Christians began, apparently, from a hint dropped by Jesus himself, when he said, "Other sheep have I which are not of this fold." This theme is developed in the prologue to the Fourth Gospel in pursuance of a most remarkable idea. It is only by the Light of Christ that men may find the way, says the prologue, but this Light is not limited to those who, by good fortune, have known Christ in the flesh or even known *about* him in the flesh. Though this Light is seen in Jesus in its full and complete manifestation, it appears, in a measure, in every son and daughter of earth. It is the Light that lighteth every man who comes into the world. Thus the Christ of experience is identical with the Christ of history, though not limited to particular historical events and particular places. It is still true that Christ is the Way, but God, in His mercy, has made the knowledge of this Way open to men in countless fashions. The enormous advantage of this conception is that it keeps the uniqueness of Christ while avoiding the blasphemy of supposing that God condemns men for mere ignorance. This makes it possible to believe that there were many Christians before Christ because they saw something of the very Light which he *was*. Who can doubt that a great measure of this Light was seen by Jeremiah or by Socrates and by millions more? There is no contradiction between the idea that God has been revealing Himself, in sundry times and sundry places, and the other idea that God has revealed Himself fully in one time and one place. Such, in any case, is the faith which is neither so vague as to be meaningless nor so narrow as to be blasphemous.

The glory of this faith, which both unites and deepens men's lives, lies in its fruits. It does for struggling men what struggling men need to have done. It is likely, for example, as some psychiatrists have suggested, that numerous people are sorely afflicted by a morbid sense of guilt, so that they are hindered in normal life and rendered incapable of peace and joy. But how is this to be cured? Of course, if analysis shows that the sense of guilt is based wholly on some trivial incident in childhood, long suppressed and supposedly forgotten, then the thing to do is to expose the source of the complex and hope that such exposure will produce cure. But what if the basis of the feeling of guilt is *not* some trivial affair? There are millions who are conscience-stricken, not because they do not understand themselves, but because they *do*. They *have* sinned; they are rightly ashamed; and the tragedy is that exposure alone does not bring a change. They come out by the same door wherein they went. They are only insulted by our advice to buck up, because that is precisely what they are powerless to do.

What would help such men and women would be a sense of genuine forgiveness. If they could know and really *feel* that the past is forgotten, that it will not be held against them, that penitence is the sufficient qualification for full forgiveness on the part of the only One who can forgive, and that they *are* truly forgiven, they would have the best that life holds in this situation. Forgiveness transcends alike the frustrating sense of continued guilt and the equally damaging sense that moral considerations are irrelevant, which is so often the popular solution. It is only in forgiveness that sin is taken seriously yet superseded. A living faith that the story of the prodigal son is the truth about the world and that the God of all the world, far from being a vindictive Judge who demands placating, is really like Christ, is exactly what millions need, even when they are supposedly superior to anything so elementary. One such man, who had not been able to walk a city block for years, and who had subjected himself to the ministrations of many healers, walked out of the pastor's study in a church on upper Fifth Avenue in New York and walked immediately for twenty blocks. He has not missed a day's work since, and the change came months ago. He found something on his knees that he had never found anywhere else.

A similar result may come to those who are bowed down by great suffering. Their deepest danger comes not from the suffering itself, but from the resultant bitterness of heart, as they think of the unfairness of their treatment in contrast with the lot of others, some of whom manifestly deserve less. The faith we have described in this chapter will not solve completely the problem of evil, but it will *illuminate* it. What may bring an abiding peace is the realization that, in their suffering, they are not alone; God, they may reasonably believe, suffers with them, for this is the deepest meaning of the cross. For many who are unjustly treated, the religious answer is really the only answer.

For the searchings of those who are weary of a meaningless freedom, which becomes so easily the bondage of self-centeredness, this faith is likewise an answer. They find that Christ offered peace, not in the sense of freedom from disturbance, but in the midst of the disturbance, and that he offered it at the price of the glad acceptance of discipline. The truth which makes men free is not a gift, but comes as a result of abiding in his word. "Take my yoke upon you," he said, "and learn of me . . . and ye shall find rest unto your souls." Our tragedy, and even our stupidity, is that we think we can have the peace without wearing the yoke.

Above all, this faith is a producer of joy. Those who listen to the apparent wisdom of Omar or any of the disciples of Epicurus soon sing a melancholy tune, but the disciples of Christ sing and shout for joy. As one of the wisest scholars of our time has said, "Joy is the strength of the people of God; it is their glory; it is their characteristic mark."[1] Why anyone could ever have supposed that the faith breeds gloom and repression is very difficult to understand. From Paul and Silas, who sang in prison at midnight, to pastors in Nazi concentration camps whose published letters could rightly bear the title *Und Lobten Gott*, the central theme has been ever the same. Listen, as to one voice out of a mighty choir, to Edward Burroughs shortly before he died in a London prison in 1662, at the age of twenty-eight:

> We received often the pouring down of the Spirit upon us and the gift of God's holy eternal Spirit, as in the days of old, and our hearts were made glad, and our tongues loosed, and our mouths opened, and we spake with new tongues as the Lord gave us utterance and as His Spirit led us, which was poured down upon us, upon Sons and Daughters.

[1] Rendel Harris.

There are truths in all the great religions, but Christianity has a certain finality in virtue of its joyousness. It is the most encouraging, the most rollicking, the least repressive and the least forbidding of all the religions of mankind. Christianity centers its faith in One who made water into wine and who laughed at the Pharisees for straining at gnats while they failed to notice that they were swallowing camels. The worst taunt against him, on the part of the very religious, was that he was a friend of publicans and sinners. It is no wonder that his followers have done so much singing. They have something to sing about.

The person who has drunk deeply of this faith is not an optimist; he does not minimize the evil that is in the world nor does he say that all men are good, which they obviously are not. Neither does he hold that things are, of themselves, necessarily getting better by some law of immanent progress. It is not "all things" that work for good, but it is *God* who works "in everything . . . with those who love him."[2] This confidence does not deny the existence of evil, but it does encourage us to believe that God is able to use even our evil acts to good ends, by His mighty power and continual care. Men, being free, can resist even the will of God in their own lives, but God can "make the wrath of men to praise Him."

We have many burdens to bear and much injustice to suffer, but if this is really God's world we cannot despair. We are not merely on our own. It is not probable that our lives were intended to be *easy*, but it *is* probable that they were intended to be rich and full, which is another matter. Of course I must al-

[2] Rom. 8:28. See especially the translation of this verse in the Revised Standard Version of the New Testament.

ways do my best and even my little contribution may be of some assistance, but I must beware of supposing that I have to do it all. God is not dead; He is working with us and for us and through us and He will win the battle. Even when we lose the way we are not lone wanderers, for He is seeking us far more truly than we are seeking Him. If all we have is our own search for the good life, our life, even in its cosmic loneliness, has a certain dignity or nobility, in spite of its pathos, but if this is God's world the pathos is transcended into glad response.

The man who sees his own life in the light of God sees himself in true perspective and ceases to be so anxious about his own little problems. He knows that this world is not centered in his puny interests, even though each person is precious in God's eyes and made in God's image. In seeing his own insignificance truly, a man thereby transcends it and rises to his true stature. Man sees his true stature, not when he looks to himself, but when he looks to God.

If the revelation of God in Christ is the true revelation, there is in the world at least one absolute in all our relativity of values. That absolute is the revolutionary love which is so rich in its meaning that the whole of the thirteenth chapter of I Corinthians is required for its definition. Those who seek to take this seriously cannot reach agreement about all its implications and specifically they cannot agree on whether loyalty to this absolute makes impossible participation in war, but all agree that it makes impossible the *hatred* of anyone. The faith which lies at the heart of the life we prize leads some to fight, in the effort to protect the weak, as they believe Christ requires, and it leads others to renounce all arms, but it leads all, who follow it sincerely, to refuse to *hate*, and that is a very great step indeed.

We believe love is a moral absolute because it reflects the nature of God. Genuine religion thus differs from philosophy or ethics, however noble and necessary they are. True religion is not man's search for the good life, important as that may be; neither is it our effort to find God, inevitable as that may be; true religion is our response to Him who seeks *us*. It is not an argument for God, but a response to God's love. If, by some historical calamity, the Christian message were lost, the essence of it could be recovered, providing we could keep only two passages, the fifteenth chapter of Luke and the eighth chapter of Romans. The one passage would give us the conception of the seeking Father, who goes out to meet the penitent child, while the other would place this fundamental insight in a cosmic setting. Together they give a reason for the belief in the infinite value of each individual and the antidote to all tyranny.

When we are doing our best to help men help themselves with the problems of living, there is no point at which we feel more powerless than in our attempt to give them courage in the face of the loss of those whom they prize more than life itself. But if, with full confidence, we can point these people to the love of God, the situation is utterly changed. Apart from the life and love of God any talk of the life everlasting is really meaningless, but once our faith in God is sure, then the conviction that death does not end all comes as a corollary. If this is really God's world, then we are under His care whether we live or whether we die. If God is, and if He is like Christ, then the problem of evil, instead of being principally a barrier to faith, becomes one of the chief reasons for believing in the conscious survival of personality after the death of the body. Since many are unfairly treated *here*, then it is evident that God's goodness is frustrated and defeated, *unless* there is a beyond. But we cannot believe that His goodness *is* permanently frustrated and defeated. Therefore there must be a future life, beyond our human ability to visualize or even imagine, in which God preserves and purifies that which here only begins. The noblest product of the millenniums of turmoil in the universe, so far as we know, is the personal individual. If individuality should be lost by the mere decay of our organic system, then what appears to be the divine purpose would be frustrated at the moment when something like victory is at last in view. That this could be the whole truth about life is so unbelievable that we must reject it as fantastic.

The faith does not tell us exactly what happens after death, either to ourselves or to those whom we love, but it is not such knowledge that we require. It is enough to know that, in our sorrow and loneliness, God cares and that God still reigns. We do not need to know the details of heaven, which may be as much beyond our grasp as poetry is beyond the grasp of an animal, but it is enough to know that we cannot drift "beyond His love and care."

This is the ultimate reason why, in the light of faith, we can sing with joy, even at the death of the young and promising. Much as we miss the ones we have lost, we can rejoice that they have found their true home in the love of God. Plato gave one of the finest of all previsions of the mood implicit in the gospel when, in the *Phaedo*, he gave us a passage wherein the dying

Socrates compares himself to the prophetic birds that are sacred to Apollo:

For they, when they perceive that they must die, having sung all their life long, *do then sing more than ever*, rejoicing in the thought that they are about to go away to the god whose ministers they are. For because they are sacred to Apollo they have the gift of prophecy, and anticipate the good things of another world; wherefore they sing and rejoice on that day more than ever they did before.[3]

Life is essentially a journey. It is of the essence of reality that it should be process, and it is of the essence of our life that we should walk. We have many dangers as we walk, for the bypaths are many and some of them lead to dead ends. It is very hard to know whether we are veritably on the high road, and that is why we must help one another. Each, as he journeys, keeps asking the way and watching for hints dropped by those who may have walked the same path, either long ago or in recent times. Sometimes we are forced to retrace our steps and frequently we find the pathway rough.

What we most need is some landmark of which we can be sure. This will not relieve us of the necessity of further searching, but it will assure us that we are moving in the right direction. Like Descartes, we are willing to engage in systematic doubt in order to avoid continual deception, but in this we always hope to find something of which we can be certain. Being finite men we can never have absolute certainty or infallibility, and in this regard the Cartesian effort was doomed to failure, but we may, if we are fortunate, find something of which we are so deeply persuaded that we are willing to stake

[3] *Phaedo*, 84 D.

our lives upon it. Such faith is not certainty or credulity, but courageous trust.

Is there anything, in this world of doubt and probability, that you verily believe, and by which you are willing to abide though the heavens fall? There is one such in my life, perhaps the only one, but one such is sufficient. It was given marvelous expression long ago by a superlatively gifted man who supported himself by making tents, but who found both meaning and joy in his life because he was utterly dedicated to one particular cause. His words were these:

For I am persuaded, that neither death, nor life, nor angels, nor principalities, nor powers, nor things present, nor things to come, nor height, nor depth, nor any other creature, shall be able to separate us from the love of God, which is in Christ Jesus our Lord.

It is no wonder that the people to whom these words were written were called those of the Way. We cannot see very far into the darkness of the future and the prospects are not really bright, but it is something if, together, we find the road.